Mr. Justice Raffles

Mr. Justice Raffles
E.W. Hornung

MINT EDITIONS

Mr. Justice Raffles was first published in 1909.

This edition published by Mint Editions 2021.

ISBN 9781513280660 | E-ISBN 9781513285689

Published by Mint Editions®

 **MINT
EDITIONS**

minteditionbooks.com

Publishing Director: Jennifer Newens
Design & Production: Rachel Lopez Metzger
Project Manager: Micaela Clark
Typesetting: Westchester Publishing Services

Contents

I

An Inaugural Banquet

Raffles had vanished from the face of the town, and even I had no conception of his whereabouts until he cabled to me to meet the 7.31 at Charing Cross next night. That was on the Tuesday before the 'Varsity match, or a full fortnight after his mysterious disappearance. The telegram was from Carlsbad, of all places for Raffles of all men! Of course there was only one thing that could possibly have taken so rare a specimen of physical fitness to any such pernicious spot. But to my horror he emerged from the train, on the Wednesday evening, a cadaverous caricature of the splendid person I had gone to meet.

"Not a word, my dear Bunny, till I have bitten British beef!" said he, in tones as hollow as his cheeks. "No, I'm not going to stop to clear my baggage now. You can do that for me to-morrow, Bunny, like a dear good pal."

"Any time you like," said I, giving him my arm. "But where shall we dine? Kellner's? Neapolo's? The Carlton or the Club?"

But Raffles shook his head at one and all.

"I don't want to dine at all," he said. "I know what I want!"

And he led the way from the station, stopping once to gloat over the sunset across Trafalgar Square, and again to inhale the tarry scent of the warm wood-paving, which was perfume to his nostrils as the din of its traffic was music to his ears, before we came to one of those political palaces which permit themselves to be included in the list of ordinary clubs. Raffles, to my surprise, walked in as though the marble hall belonged to him, and as straight as might be to the grill-room where white-capped cooks were making things hiss upon a silver grill. He did not consult me as to what we were to have. He had made up his mind about that in the train. But he chose the fillet steaks himself, he insisted on seeing the kidneys, and had a word to say about the fried potatoes, and the Welsh rarebit that was to follow. And all this was as uncharacteristic of the normal Raffles (who was least fastidious at the table) as the sigh with which he dropped into the chair opposite mine, and crossed his arms upon the cloth.

"I didn't know you were a member of this place," said I, feeling really rather shocked at the discovery, but also that it was a safer subject for me to open than that of his late mysterious movements.

"There are a good many things you don't know about me, Bunny," said he wearily. "Did you know I was in Carlsbad, for instance?"

"Of course I didn't."

"Yet you remember the last time we sat down together?"

"You mean that night we had supper at the Savoy?"

"It's only three weeks ago, Bunny."

"It seems months to me."

"And years to me!" cried Raffles. "But surely you remember that lost tribesman at the next table, with the nose like the village pump, and the wife with the emerald necklace?"

"I should think I did," said I; "you mean the great Dan Levy, otherwise Mr. Shylock? Why, you told me all about him, A. J."

"Did I? Then you may possibly recollect that the Shylocks were off to Carlsbad the very next day. It was the old man's last orgy before his annual cure, and he let the whole room know it. Ah, Bunny, I can sympathise with the poor brute now!"

"But what on earth took you there, old fellow?"

"Can you ask? Have you forgotten how you saw the emeralds under their table when they'd gone, and how *I* forgot myself and ran after them with the best necklace I'd handled since the days of Lady Melrose?"

I shook my head, partly in answer to his question, but partly also over a piece of perversity which still rankled in my recollection. But now I was prepared for something even more perverse.

"You were quite right," continued Raffles, recalling my recriminations at the time; "it was a rotten thing to do. It was also the action of a tactless idiot, since anybody could have seen that a heavy necklace like that couldn't have dropped off without the wearer's knowledge."

"You don't mean to say she dropped it on purpose?" I exclaimed with more interest, for I suddenly foresaw the remainder of his tale.

"I do," said Raffles. "The poor old pet did it deliberately when stooping to pick up something else; and all to get it stolen and delay their trip to Carlsbad, where her swab of a husband makes her do the cure with him."

I said I always felt that we had failed to fulfil an obvious destiny in the matter of those emeralds; and there was something touching in the way Raffles now sided with me against himself.

"But I saw it the moment I had yanked them up," said he, "and heard that fat swine curse his wife for dropping them. He told her she'd done it on purpose, too; he hit the nail on the head all right; but it was her poor head, and that showed me my unworthy impulse in its true light, Bunny. I didn't need your reproaches to make me realise what a skunk I'd been all round. I saw that the necklace was morally yours, and there was one clear call for me to restore it to you by hook, crook, or barrel. I left for Carlsbad as soon after its wrongful owners as prudence permitted."

"Admirable!" said I, overjoyed to find old Raffles by no means in such bad form as he looked. "But not to have taken me with you, A. J., that's the unkind cut I can't forgive."

"My dear Bunny, you couldn't have borne it," said Raffles solemnly. "The cure would have killed you; look what it's done to me."

"Don't tell me you went through with it!" I rallied him.

"Of course I did, Bunny. I played the game like a prayer-book."

"But why, in the name of all that's wanton?"

"You don't know Carlsbad, or you wouldn't ask. The place is squirming with spies and humbugs. If I had broken the rules one of the prize humbugs laid down for me I should have been spotted in a tick by a spy, and bowled out myself for a spy and a humbug rolled into one. Oh, Bunny, if old man Dante were alive to-day I should commend him to that sink of salubrity for the redraw material of another and a worse Inferno!"

The steaks had arrived, smoking hot, with a kidney apiece and lashings of fried potatoes. And for a divine interval (as it must have been to him) Raffles's only words were to the waiter, and referred to successive tankards of bitter, with the superfluous rider that the man who said we couldn't drink beer was a liar. But indeed I never could myself, and only achieved the impossible in this case out of sheer sympathy with Raffles. And eventually I had my reward, in such a recital of malignant privation as I cannot trust myself to set down in any words but his.

"No, Bunny, you couldn't have borne it for half a week; you'd have looked like that all the time!" quoth Raffles. I suppose my face had fallen (as it does too easily) at his aspersion on my endurance. "Cheer up, my man; that's better," he went on, as I did my best. "But it was no smiling matter out there. No one does smile after the first week; your sense of humour is the first thing the cure eradicates. There was a hunting man at my hotel, getting his weight down to ride a special thoroughbred, and no doubt a cheery dog at home; but, poor devil, he hadn't much chance of good cheer there! Miles and miles on his poor feet before breakfast; mud-poultices all the morning; and not the semblance of a drink all day, except some aerated muck called Gieshübler. He was allowed to lap that up an hour after meals, when his tongue would be hanging out of his mouth. We went to the same weighing machine at cock-crow, and though he looked quite good-natured once when I caught him asleep in his chair, I have known him tear up his weight ticket when he had gained an ounce or two instead of losing one or two pounds. We began by taking our walks together, but his conversation used to get so physically introspective that one couldn't get in a word about one's own works edgeways."

"But there was nothing wrong with your works," I reminded Raffles; he shook his head as one who was not so sure.

"Perhaps not at first, but the cure soon sees to that! I closed in like a concertina, Bunny, and I only hope I shall be able to pull out like one. You see, it's the custom of the accursed place for one to telephone for a doctor the moment one arrives. I consulted the hunting man, who of course recommended his own in order to make sure of a companion on the rack. The old arch-humbug was down upon me in ten minutes, examining me from crown to heel, and made the most unblushing report upon my general condition. He said I had a liver! I'll swear I hadn't before I went to Carlsbad, but I shouldn't be a bit surprised if I'd brought one back."

And he tipped his tankard with a solemn face, before falling to work upon the Welsh rarebit which had just arrived.

"It looks like gold, and it's golden eating," said poor old Raffles. "I only wish that sly dog of a doctor could see me at it! He had the nerve to make me write out my own health-warrant, and it was so like my friend the hunting man's that it dispelled his settled gloom for the whole of that evening. We used to begin our drinking day at the same well of German damnably defiled, and we paced the same colonnade to the blare of the same well-fed band. That wasn't a joke, Bunny; it's not a thing to joke about; mud-poultices and dry meals, with teetotal poisons in between, were to be my portion too. You stiffen your lip at that, eh, Bunny? I told you that you never would or could have stood it; but it was the only game to play for the Emerald Stakes. It kept one above suspicion all the time. And then I didn't mind that part as much as you would, or as my hunting pal did; he was driven to fainting at the doctor's place one day, in the forlorn hope of a toothful of brandy to bring him round. But all he got was a glass of cheap Marsala."

"But did you win those stakes after all?"

"Of course I did, Bunny," said Raffles below his breath, and with a look that I remembered later. "But the waiters are listening as it is, and I'll tell you the rest some other time. I suppose you know what brought me back so soon?"

"Hadn't you finished your cure?"

"Not by three good days. I had the satisfaction of a row royal with the Lord High Humbug to account for my hurried departure. But, as a matter of fact, if Teddy Garland hadn't got his Blue at the eleventh hour I should be at Carlsbad still."

E.M. Garland (Eton and Trinity) was the Cambridge wicketkeeper, and one of the many young cricketers who owed a good deal to Raffles. They had made friends in some country-house week, and foregathered afterward in town, where the young fellow's father had a house at which Raffles became a constant guest. I am afraid I was a little prejudiced both against the father, a retired brewer whom I had never met, and the son whom I did meet once or twice at the Albany. Yet I could quite understand the mutual attraction between Raffles and this much younger man; indeed he was a mere boy, but like so many of his school he seemed to have a knowledge of the world beyond his years, and withal such a spontaneous spring of sweetness and charm as neither knowledge nor experience could sensibly pollute. And yet I had a shrewd suspicion that wild oats had been somewhat freely sown, and that it was Raffles who had stepped in and taken the sower in hand, and turned him into the stuff of which Blues are made. At least I knew that no one could be sounder friend or saner counsellor to any young fellow in need of either. And many there must be to bear me out in their hearts; but they did not know their Raffles as I knew mine; and if they say that was why they thought so much of him, let them have patience, and at last they shall hear something that need not make them think the less.

"I couldn't let poor Teddy keep at Lord's," explained Raffles, "and me not there to egg him on! You see, Bunny, I taught him a thing or two in those little matches we played together last August. I take a fatherly interest in the child."

"You must have done him a lot of good," I suggested, "in every way."

Raffles looked up from his bill and asked me what I meant. I saw he was not pleased with my remark, but I was not going back on it.

"Well, I should imagine you had straightened him out a bit, if you ask me."

"I didn't ask you, Bunny, that's just the point!" said Raffles. And I watched him tip the waiter without the least *arrière-pensée* on either side.

"After all," said I, on our way down the marble stair, "you have told me a good deal about the lad. I remember once hearing you say he had a lot of debts, for example."

"So I was afraid," replied Raffles, frankly; "and between ourselves, I offered to finance him before I went abroad. Teddy wouldn't hear of it; that hot young blood of his was up at the thought, though he was perfectly delightful in what he said. So don't jump to rotten conclusions, Bunny, but stroll up to the Albany and have a drink."

And when we had reclaimed our hats and coats, and lit our Sullivans in the hall, out we marched as though I were now part-owner of the place with Raffles.

"That," said I, to effect a thorough change of conversation, since I felt at one with all the world, "is certainly the finest grill in Europe."

"That's why we went there, Bunny."

"But must I say I was rather surprised to find you a member of a place where you tip the waiter and take a ticket for your hat!"

I was not surprised, however, to hear Raffles defend his own caravanserai.

"I would go a step further," he remarked, "and make every member show his badge as they do at Lord's."

"But surely the porter knows the members by sight?"

"Not he! There are far too many thousands of them."

"I should have thought he must."

"And I know he doesn't."

"Well, you ought to know, A.J., since you're a member yourself."

"On the contrary, my dear Bunny, I happen to know because I never was one!"

II

"His Own Familiar Friend"

How we laughed as we turned into Whitehall! I began to feel I had been wrong about Raffles after all, and that enhanced my mirth. Surely this was the old gay rascal, and it was by some uncanny feat of his stupendous will that he had appeared so haggard on the platform. In the London lamplight that he loved so well, under a starry sky of an almost theatrical blue, he looked another man already. If such a change was due to a few draughts of bitter beer and a few ounces of fillet steak, then I felt I was the brewers' friend and the vegetarians' foe for life. Nevertheless I could detect a serious side to my companion's mood, especially when he spoke once more of Teddy Garland, and told me that he had cabled to him also before leaving Carlsbad. And I could not help wondering, with a discreditable pang, whether his intercourse with that honest lad could have bred in Raffles a remorse for his own misdeeds, such as I myself had often tried, but always failed, to produce.

So we came to the Albany in sober frame, for all our recent levity, thinking at least no evil for once in our lawless lives. And there was our good friend Barraclough, the porter, to salute and welcome us in the courtyard.

"There's a gen'leman writing you a letter upstairs," said he to Raffles. "It's Mr. Garland, sir, so I took him up."

"Teddy!" cried Raffles, and took the stairs two at a time.

I followed rather heavily. It was not jealousy, but I did feel rather critical of this mushroom intimacy. So I followed up, feeling that the evening was spoilt for me—and God knows I was right! Not till my dying day shall I forget the tableau that awaited me in those familiar rooms. I see it now as plainly as I see the problem picture of the year, which lies in wait for one in all the illustrated papers; indeed, it was a problem picture itself in flesh and blood.

Raffles had opened his door as only Raffles could open doors, with the boyish thought of giving the other boy a fright; and young Garland had very naturally started up from the bureau, where he was writing, at the sudden clap of his own name behind him. But that was the last of his natural actions. He did not advance to grasp Raffles by the hand;

there was no answering smile of welcome on the fresh young face which used to remind me of the Phoebus in Guido's Aurora, with its healthy pink and bronze, and its hazel eye like clear amber. The pink faded before our gaze, the bronze turned a sickly sallow; and there stood Teddy Garland as if glued to the bureau behind him, clutching its edge with all his might. I can see his knuckles gleaming like ivory under the back of each sunburnt hand.

"What is it? What are you hiding?" demanded Raffles. His love for the lad had rung out in his first greeting; his puzzled voice was still jocular and genial, but the other's attitude soon strangled that. All this time I had been standing in vague horror on the threshold; now Raffles beckoned me in and switched on more light. It fell full upon a ghastly and a guilty face, that yet stared bravely in the glare. Raffles locked the door behind us, put the key in his pocket, and strode over to the desk.

No need to report their first broken syllables: enough that it was no note young Garland was writing, but a cheque which he was laboriously copying into Raffles's cheque-book, from an old cheque abstracted from a pass-book with A. J. RAFFLES in gilt capitals upon its brown leather back. Raffles had only that year opened a banking account, and I remembered his telling me how thoroughly he meant to disregard the instructions on his cheque-book by always leaving it about to advertise the fact. And this was the result. A glance convicted his friend of criminal intent: a sheet of notepaper lay covered with trial signatures. Yet Raffles could turn and look with infinite pity upon the miserable youth who was still looking defiantly on him.

"My poor chap!" was all he said.

And at that the broken boy found the tongue of a hoarse and quavering old man.

"Won't you hand me over and be done with it?" he croaked. "Must you torture me yourself?"

It was all I could do to refrain from putting in my word, and telling the fellow it was not for him to ask questions. Raffles merely inquired whether he had thought it all out before.

"God knows I hadn't, A. J.! I came up to write you a note, I swear I did," said Garland with a sudden sob.

"No need to swear it," returned Raffles, actually smiling. "Your word's quite good enough for me."

"God bless you for that, after this!" the other choked, in terrible disorder now.

"It was pretty obvious," said Raffles reassuringly.

"Was it? Are you sure? You do remember offering me a cheque last month, and my refusing it?"

"Why, of course I do!" cried Raffles, with such spontaneous heartiness that I could see he had never thought of it since mentioning the matter to me at our meal. What I could not see was any reason for such conspicuous relief, or the extenuating quality of a circumstance which seemed to me rather to aggravate the offence.

"I have regretted that refusal ever since," young Garland continued very simply. "It was a mistake at the time, but this week of all weeks it's been a tragedy. Money I must have; I'll tell you why directly. When I got your wire last night it seemed as though my wretched prayers had been answered. I was going to someone else this morning, but I made up my mind to wait for you instead. You were the one I really could turn to, and yet I refused your great offer a month ago. But you said you would be back to-night; and you weren't here when I came. I telephoned and found that the train had come in all right, and that there wasn't another until the morning. Tomorrow morning's my limit, and to-morrow's the match." He stopped as he saw what Raffles was doing. "Don't, Raffles, I don't deserve it!" he added in fresh distress.

But Raffles had unlocked the tantalus and found a syphon in the corner cupboard, and it was a very yellow bumper that he handed to the guilty youth.

"Drink some," he said, "or I won't listen to another word."

"I'm going to be ruined before the match begins. I am!" the poor fellow insisted, turning to me when Raffles shook his head. "And it'll break my father's heart, and—and—"

I thought he had worse still to tell us, he broke off in such despair; but either he changed his mind, or the current of his thoughts set inward in spite of him, for when he spoke again it was to offer us both a further explanation of his conduct.

"I only came up to leave a line for Raffles," he said to me, "in case he did get back in time. It was the porter himself who fixed me up at that bureau. He'll tell you how many times I had called before. And then I saw before my nose in one pigeon-hole your cheque-book, Raffles, and your pass-book bulging with old cheques."

"And as I wasn't back to write one for you," said Raffles, "you wrote it for me. And quite right, too!"

"Don't laugh at me!" cried the boy, his lost colour rushing back. And he looked at me again as though my long face hurt him less than the sprightly sympathy of his friend.

"I'm not laughing, Teddy," replied Raffles kindly. "I was never more serious in my life. It was playing the friend to come to me at all in your fix, but it was the act of a real good pal to draw on me behind my back rather than let me feel I'd ruined you by not turning up in time. You may shake your head as hard as you like, but I never was paid a higher compliment."

And the consummate casuist went on working a congenial vein until a less miserable sinner might have been persuaded that he had done nothing really dishonourable; but young Garland had the grace neither to make nor to accept any excuse for his own conduct. I never heard a man more down upon himself, or confession of error couched in stronger terms; and yet there was something so sincere and ingenuous in his remorse, something that Raffles and I had lost so long ago, that in our hearts I am sure we took his follies more seriously than our own crimes. But foolish he indeed had been, if not criminally foolish as he said. It was the old story of the prodigal son of an indulgent father. There had been, as I suspected, a certain amount of youthful riot which the influence of Raffles had already quelled; but there had also been much reckless extravagance, of which Raffles naturally knew less, since your scapegrace is constitutionally quicker to confess himself as such than as a fool. Suffice it that this one had thrown himself on his father's generosity, only to find that the father himself was in financial straits.

"What!" cried Raffles, "with that house on his hands?"

"I knew it would surprise you," said Teddy Garland. "I can't understand it myself; he gave me no particulars, but the mere fact was enough for me. I simply couldn't tell my father everything after that. He wrote me a cheque for all I did own up to, but I could see it was such a tooth that I swore I'd never come on him to pay another farthing. And I never will!"

The boy took a sip from his glass, for his voice had faltered, and then he paused to light another cigarette, because the last had gone out between his fingers. So sensitive and yet so desperate was the blonde young face, with the creased forehead and the nervous mouth, that I saw Raffles look another way until the match was blown out.

"But at the time I might have done worse, and did," said Teddy, "a thousand times! I went to the Jews. That's the whole trouble. There were more debts—debts of honour—and to square up I went to the Jews. It was only a matter of two or three hundred to start with; but you may know, though I didn't, what a snowball the smallest sum becomes in the hands of those devils. I borrowed three hundred and signed a promissory note for four hundred and fifty-six."

"Only fifty per cent!" said Raffles. "You got off cheap if the percentage was per annum."

"Wait a bit! It was by way of being even more reasonable than that. The four hundred and fifty-six was repayable in monthly instalments of twenty quid, and I kept them up religiously until the sixth payment fell due. That was soon after Christmas, when one's always hard up, and for the first time I was a day or two late—not more, mind you; yet what do you suppose happened? My cheque was returned, and the whole blessed balance demanded on the nail!"

Raffles was following intently, with that complete concentration which was a signal force in his equipment. His face no longer changed at anything he heard; it was as strenuously attentive as that of any judge upon the bench. Never had I clearer vision of the man he might have been but for the kink in his nature which had made him what he was.

"The promissory note was for four-fifty-six," said he, "and this sudden demand was for the lot less the hundred you had paid?"

"That's it."

"What did you do?" I asked, not to seem behind Raffles in my grasp of the case.

"Told them to take my instalment or go to blazes for the rest!"

"And they?"

"Absolutely drop the whole thing until this very week, and then come down on me for—what do you suppose?"

"Getting on for a thousand," said Raffles after a moment's thought.

"Nonsense!" I cried. Garland looked astonished too.

"Raffles knows all about it," said he. "Seven hundred was the actual figure. I needn't tell you I have given the bounders a wide berth since the day I raised the wind; but I went and had it out with them over this. And half the seven hundred is for default interest, I'll trouble you, from the beginning of January down to date!"

"Had you agreed to that?"

"Not to my recollection, but there it was as plain as a pikestaff on my promissory note. A halfpenny in the shilling per week over and above everything else when the original interest wasn't forthcoming."

"Printed or written on your note of hand?"

"Printed—printed small, I needn't tell you—but quite large enough for me to read when I signed the cursed bond. In fact I believe I did read it; but a halfpenny a week! Who could ever believe it would mount up like that? But it does; it's right enough, and the long and short of it is that unless I pay up by twelve o'clock to-morrow the governor's to be called in to say whether he'll pay up for me or see me made a bankrupt under his nose. Twelve o'clock, when the match begins! Of course they know that, and are trading on it. Only this evening I had the most insolent ultimatum, saying it was my 'dead and last chance.'"

"So then you came round here?"

"I was coming in any case. I wish I'd shot myself first!"

"My dear fellow, it was doing me proud; don't let us lose our sense of proportion, Teddy."

But young Garland had his face upon his hand, and once more he was the miserable man who had begun brokenly to unfold the history of his shame. The unconscious animation produced by the mere unloading of his heart, the natural boyish slang with which his tale had been freely garnished, had faded from his face, had died upon his lips. Once more he was a soul in torments of despair and degradation; and yet once more did the absence of the abject in man and manner redeem him from the depths of either. In these moments of reaction he was pitiful, but not contemptible, much less unlovable. Indeed, I could see the qualities that had won the heart of Raffles as I had never seen them before. There is a native nobility not to be destroyed by a single descent into the ignoble, an essential honesty too bright and brilliant to be dimmed by incidental dishonour; and both remained to the younger man, in the eyes of the other two, who were even then determining to preserve in him all that they themselves had lost. The thought came naturally enough to me. And yet I may well have derived it from a face that for once was easy to read, a clear-cut face that had never looked so sharp in profile, or, to my knowledge, half so gentle in expression.

"And what about these Jews?" asked Raffles at length.

"There's really only one."

"Are we to guess his name?"

"No, I don't mind telling you. It's Dan Levy."

"Of course it is!" cried Raffles with a nod for me. "Our Mr. Shylock in all his glory!"

Teddy snatched his face from his hands.

"You don't know him, do you?"

"I might almost say I know him at home," said Raffles. "But as a matter of fact I met him abroad."

Teddy was on his feet.

"But do you know him well enough—"

"Certainly. I'll see him in the morning. But I ought to have the receipts for the various instalments you have paid, and perhaps that letter saying it was your last chance."

"Here they all are," said Garland, producing a bulky envelope. "But of course I'll come with you—"

"Of course you'll do nothing of the kind, Teddy! I won't have your eye put out for the match by that old ruffian, and I'm not going to let you sit up all night either. Where are you staying, my man?"

"Nowhere yet. I left my kit at the club. I was going out home if I'd caught you early enough."

"Stout fellow! You stay here."

"My dear old man, I couldn't think of it," said Teddy gratefully.

"My dear young man, I don't care whether you think of it or not. Here you stay, and moreover you turn in at once. I can fix you up with all you want, and Barraclough shall bring your kit round before you're awake."

"But you haven't got a bed, Raffles?"

"You shall have mine. I hardly ever go to bed—do I, Bunny?"

"I've seldom seen you there," said I.

"But you were travelling all last night?"

"And straight through till this evening, and I sleep all the time in a train," said Raffles. "I hardly opened an eye all day; if I turned in to-night I shouldn't get a wink."

"Well, I shan't either," said the other hopelessly. "I've forgotten how to sleep!"

"Wait till I learn you!" said Raffles, and went into the inner room and lit it up.

"I'm terribly sorry about it all," whispered young Garland, turning to me as though we were old friends now.

"And I'm sorry for you," said I from my heart. "I know what it is."

Garland was still staring when Raffles returned with a tiny bottle from which he was shaking little round black things into his left palm.

"Clean sheets yawning for you, Teddy," said he. "And now take two of these, and one more spot of whisky, and you'll be asleep in ten minutes."

"What are they?"

"Somnol. The latest thing out, and quite the best."

"But won't they give me a frightful head?"

"Not a bit of it; you'll be as right as rain ten minutes after you wake up. And you needn't leave this before eleven to-morrow morning, because you don't want a knock at the nets, do you?"

"I ought to have one," said Teddy seriously. But Raffles laughed him to scorn.

"They're not playing you for runs, my man, and I shouldn't run any risks with those hands. Remember all the chances they're going to lap up to-morrow, and all the byes they've not got to let!"

And Raffles had administered his opiate before the patient knew much more about it; next minute he was shaking hands with me, and the minute after that Raffles went in to put out his light. He was gone some little time; and I remember leaning out of the window in order not to overhear the conversation in the next room. The night was nearly as fine as ever. The starry ceiling over the Albany Courtyard was only less beautifully blue than when Raffles and I had come in a couple of hours ago. The traffic in Piccadilly came as crisply to the ear as on a winter's night of hard frost. It was a night of wine, and sparkling wine, and the day at Lord's must surely be a day of nectar. I could not help wondering whether any man had ever played in the University match with such a load upon his soul as E.M. Garland was taking to his forced slumbers; and then whether any heavy-laden soul had ever hit upon two such brother confessors as Raffles and myself!

III

Council of War

Raffles was humming a snatch of something too choice for me to recognise when I drew in my head from the glorious night. The folding-doors were shut, and the grandfather's clock on one side of them made it almost midnight. Raffles would not stop his tune for me, but he pointed to the syphon and decanter, and I replenished my glass. He had a glass beside him also, which was less usual, but he did not sit down beside his glass; he was far too fidgety for that; even bothering about a pair of pictures which had changed places under some zealous hand in his absence, or rather two of Mr. Hollyer's fine renderings of Watts and Burne-Jones of which I had never seen Raffles take the slightest notice before. But it seemed that they must hang where he had hung them, and for once I saw them hanging straight. The books had also suffered from good intentions; he gave them up with a shrug. Archives and arcana he tested or examined, and so a good many minutes passed without a word. But when he stole back into the inner room, after waiting a little at the folding-doors, there was still some faint strain upon his lips; it was only when he returned, shutting the door none too quietly behind him, that he stopped humming and spoke out with a grimmer face than he had worn all night.

"That boy's in a bigger hole than he thinks. But we must pull him out between us before play begins. It's one clear call for us, Bunny!"

"Is it a bigger hole than you thought?" I asked, thinking myself of the conversation which I had managed not to overhear.

"I don't say that, Bunny, though I never should have dreamt of his old father being in one too. I own I can't understand that. They live in a regular country house in the middle of Kensington, and there are only the two of them. But I've given Teddy my word not to go to the old man for the money, so it's no use talking about it."

But apparently it was what they had been talking about behind the folding-doors; it only surprised me to see how much Raffles took it to heart.

"So you have made up your mind to raise the money elsewhere?"

"Before that lad in there opens his eyes."

"Is he asleep already?"

"Like the dead," said Raffles, dropping into his chair and drinking thoughtfully; "and so he will be till we wake him up. It's a ticklish experiment, Bunny, but even a splitting head for the first hour's play is better than a sleepless night; I've tried both, so I ought to know. I shouldn't even wonder if he did himself more than justice to-morrow; one often does when just less than fit; it takes off that dangerous edge of over-keenness which so often cuts one's own throat."

"But what do you think of it all, A.J.?"

"Not so much worse than I let him think I thought."

"But you must have been amazed?"

"I am past amazement at the worst thing the best of us ever does, and contrariwise of course. Your rich man proves a pauper, and your honest man plays the knave; we're all of us capable of every damned thing. But let us thank our stars and Teddy's that we got back just when we did."

"Why at that moment?"

Raffles produced the unfinished cheque, shook his head over it, and sent it fluttering across to me.

"Was there ever such a childish attempt? They'd have kept him in the bank while they sent for the police. If ever you want to play this game, Bunny, you must let me coach you up a bit."

"But it was never one of your games, A.J.!"

"Only incidentally once or twice; it never appealed to me," said Raffles, sending expanding circlets of smoke to crown the girls on the Golden Stair that was no longer tilted in a leaning tower. "No, Bunny, an occasional *exeat* at school is my modest record as a forger, though I admit that augured ill. Do you remember how I left my cheque-book about on purpose for what's happened? To be sinned against instead of sinning, in all the papers, would have set one up as an honest man for life. I thought, God forgive me, of poor old Barraclough or somebody of that kind. And to think it should be 'the friend in whom my soul confided'! Not that I ever did confide in him, Bunny, much as I love this lad."

Despite the tense of that last statement, it was the old Raffles who was speaking now, the incisively cynical old Raffles that I still knew the best, the Raffles of the impudent quotations and jaunty *jeux d'esprit*. This Raffles only meant half he said—but had generally done the other half! I met his mood by reminding him (out of his own *Whitaker*) that the sun rose at 3.51, in case he thought of breaking in anywhere that night. I had the honour of making Raffles smile.

"I did think of it, Bunny," said he. "But there's only one crib that we could crack in decency for this money; and our Mr. Shylock's is not the sort of city that Caesar himself would have taken *ex itinere*. It's a case for the *testudo* and all the rest of it. You must remember that I've been there, Bunny; at least I've visited his 'moving tent,' if one may jump from an ancient to an 'Ancient and Modern.' And if that was as impregnable as I found it, his permanent citadel must be perched upon the very rock of defence!"

"You must tell me about that, Raffles," said I, tiring a little of his kaleidoscopic metaphors. Let him be as allusive as he liked when there was no risky work on hand, and I was his lucky and delighted audience till all hours of the night or morning. But for a deed of darkness I wanted fewer fireworks, a steadier light from his intellectual lantern. And yet these were the very moments that inspired his pyrotechnic displays.

"Oh, I shall tell you all right," said Raffles. "But just now the next few hours are of more importance than the last few weeks. Of course Shylock's the man for our money; but knowing our tribesmen as I do, I think we had better begin by borrowing it like simple Christians."

"Then we have it to pay back again."

"And that's the psychological moment for raiding our 'miser's sunless coffers'—if he happens to have any. It will give us time to find out."

"But he doesn't keep open office all night," I objected.

"But he opens at nine o'clock in the morning," said Raffles, "to catch the early stockbroker who would rather be bled than hammered."

"Who told you that?"

"Our Mrs. Shylock."

"You must have made great friends with her?"

"More in pity than for the sake of secrets."

"But you went where the secrets were?"

"And she gave them away wholesale."

"She would," I said, "to you."

"She told me a lot about the impending libel action."

"Shylock *v. Fact?* "

"Yes; it's coming on before the vacation, you know."

"So I saw in some paper."

"But you know what it's all about, Bunny?"

"No, I don't."

"Another old rascal, the Maharajah of Hathipur, and his perfectly fabulous debts. It seems he's been in our Mr. Shylock's clutches for years, but instead of taking his pound of flesh he's always increasing the amount. Of course that's the whole duty of money-lenders, but now they say the figure runs well into six. No one has any sympathy with that old heathen; he's said to have been a pal of Nana's before the Mutiny, and in it up to the neck he only saved by turning against his own lot in time; in any case it's the pot and the kettle so far as moral colour is concerned. But I believe it's an actual fact that syndicates have been formed to buy up the black man's debts and take a reasonable interest, only the dirty white man always gets to windward of the syndicate. They're on the point of bringing it off, when old Levy inveigles the nigger into some new Oriental extravagance. *Fact* has exposed the whole thing, and printed blackmailing letters which Shylock swears are forgeries. That's both their cases in a philippine! The leeches told the Jew he must do his Carlsbad this year before the case came on; and the tremendous amount it's going to cost may account for his dunning old clients the moment he gets back."

"Then why should he lend to you?"

"I'm a new client, Bunny; that makes all the difference. Then we were very good pals out there."

"But you and Mrs. Shylock were better still?"

"Unbeknowns, Bunny! She used to tell me her troubles when I lent her an arm and took due care to look a martyr; my hunting friend had coarse metaphors about heavy-weights and the knacker's yard."

"And yet you came away with the poor soul's necklace?"

Raffles was tapping the chronic cigarette on the table at his elbow; he stood up to light it, as one does stand up to make the dramatic announcements of one's life, and he spoke through the flame of the match as it rose and fell between his puffs.

"No—Bunny—I did not!"

"But you told me you won the Emerald Stakes!" I cried, jumping up in my turn.

"So I did, Bunny, but I gave them back again."

"You gave yourself away to her, as she'd given him away to you?"

"Don't be a fool, Bunny," said Raffles, subsiding into his chair. "I can't tell you the whole thing now, but here are the main heads. They're at the Savoy Hotel, in Carlsbad I mean. I go to Pupp's. We meet. They stare. I come out of my British shell as the humble hero of the affair at the other Savoy. I crab my hotel. They swear by theirs. I go to see their rooms. I wait till I can get the very same thing immediately overhead on the second floor—where I can even hear the old swine cursing her from under his mud-poultice! Both suites have balconies that might have been made for me. Need I go on?"

"I wonder you weren't suspected."

"There's no end to your capacity for wonder, Bunny. I took some sweet old rags with me on purpose, carefully packed inside a decent suit, and I had the luck to pick up a foul old German cap that some peasant had cast off in the woods. I only meant to leave it on them like a card; as it was—well, I was waiting for the best barber in the place to open his shop next morning."

"What had happened?"

"A whole actful of unrehearsed effects; that's why I think twice before taking on old Shylock again. I admire him, Bunny, as a steely foeman. I look forward to another game with him on his own ground. But I must find out the pace of the wicket before I put myself on."

"I suppose you had tea with them, and all that sort of thing?"

"Gieshübler!" said Raffles with a shudder. "But I made it last as long as tea, and thought I had located the little green lamps before I took my leave. There was a japanned despatch box in one corner. 'That's the Emerald Isle,' I thought, 'I'll soon have it out of the sea. The old man won't trust 'em to the old lady after what happened in town,' I needn't tell you I knew they were there somewhere; he made her wear them even at the tragic travesty of a Carlsbad hotel dinner."

Raffles was forgetting to be laconic now. I believe he had forgotten the lad in the next room, and everything else but the breathless battle that he was fighting over again for my benefit. He told me how he waited for a dark night, and then slid down from his sitting-room balcony to the one below. And my emeralds were not in the japanned box after all; and just as he had assured himself of the fact, the folding-doors opened "as it might be these," and there stood Dan Levy "in a suit of swagger silk pyjamas."

"They gave me a sudden respect for him," continued Raffles; "it struck me, for the first time, that mud baths mightn't be the only ones he ever took. His face was as evil as ever, but he was utterly unarmed, and I was not; and yet there he stood and abused me like a pickpocket, as if there was no chance of my firing, and he didn't care whether I did or not. So I stuck my revolver nearly in his face, and pulled the hammer up and up. Good God, Bunny, if I had pulled too hard! But that made him blink a bit, and I was jolly glad to let it down again. 'Out with those emeralds,' says I in low German mugged up in case of need. Of course you realise that I was absolutely unrecognisable, a low blackguard with a blackened face. 'I don't know what you mean,' says he, 'and I'm damned if I care.' '*Das halsband*, says I, which means the necklace. 'Go to hell,' says he. But I struck myself and shook my head and then my fist at him and nodded. He laughed in my face; and upon my soul we were at a deadlock. So I pointed to the clock and held up one finger. 'I've one minute to live, old girl,' says he through the doors, 'if this rotter has the guts to shoot, and I don't think he has. Why the hell don't you get out the other way and alarm the 'ouse?' And that raised the siege, Bunny. In comes the old woman, as plucky as he was, and shoves the necklace into my left hand. I longed to refuse it. I didn't dare. And the old beast took her and shook her like a rat, until I covered him again, and swore in German that if he showed himself on the balcony for the next two minutes he'd be *ein toter Englander*! That was the other bit I'd got off pat; it was meant to mean 'a dead Englishman.' And I left the fine old girl clinging on to him, instead of him to her!"

I emptied my lungs and my glass too. Raffles took a sip himself.

"But the rope was fixed to *your* balcony, A.J.?"

"But I began by fixing the other end to theirs, and the moment I was safely up I undid my end and dropped it clear to the ground. They found it dangling all right when out they rushed together. Of course I'd picked the right ball in the way of nights; it was bone-dry as well as pitch-dark, and in five minutes I was helping the rest of the hotel to search for impossible footprints on the gravel, and to stamp out any there might conceivably have been."

"So nobody ever suspected you?"

"Not a soul, I can safely say; I was the first my victims bored with the whole yarn."

"Then why return the swag? It's an old trick of yours, Raffles, but in a case like this, with a pig like that, I confess I don't see the point."

"You forget the poor old lady, Bunny. She had a dog's life before; after that the beans he gave her weren't even fit for a dog. I loved her for her pluck in standing up to him; it beat his hollow in standing up to me; there was only one reward for her, and it was in my gift."

"But how on earth did you manage that?"

"Not by public presentation, Bunny, nor yet by taking the old dame into my confidence *more cuniculi!*"

"I suppose you returned the necklace anonymously?"

"As a low-down German burglar would be sure to do! No, Bunny, I planted it in the woods where I knew it would be found. And then I had to watch lest it was found by the wrong sort. But luckily Mr. Shylock had sprung a substantial reward, and all came right in the end. He sent his doctor to blazes, and had a buck feed and lashings on the night it was recovered. The hunting man and I were invited to the thanksgiving spread; but I wouldn't budge from the diet, and he was ashamed to unless I did. It made a coolness between us, and now I doubt if we shall ever have that enormous dinner we used to talk about to celebrate our return from a living tomb."

But I was not interested in that shadowy fox-hunter. "Dan Levy's a formidable brute to tackle," said I at length, and none too buoyantly.

"That's a very true observation, Bunny; it's also exactly why I so looked forward to tackling him. It ought to be the kind of conflict that the halfpenny press have learnt to call Homeric."

"Are you thinking of to-morrow, or of when it comes to robbing Peter to pay Peter?"

"Excellent, Bunny!" cried Raffles, as though I had made a shot worthy of his willow. "How the small hours brighten us up!" He drew the curtains and displayed a window like a child's slate with the sashes ruled across it. "You perceive how we have tired the stars with talking, and cleaned them from the sky! The mellifluous Heraclitus can have been no sitter up o' nights, or his pal wouldn't have boasted about tiring the sun by our methods. What a lot the two old pets must have missed!"

"You haven't answered my question," said I resignedly. "Nor have you told me how you propose to go to work to raise this money in the first instance."

"If you like to light another Sullivan," said Raffles, "and mix yourself another very small and final one, I can tell you now, Bunny."

And tell me he did.

IV

"Our Mr. Shylock"

I have often wondered in what pause or phase of our conversation Raffles hit upon the plan which we duly carried out; for we had been talking incessantly, since his arrival about eight o'clock at night, until two in the morning. Yet that which we discussed between two and three was what we actually did between nine and ten, with the single exception necessitated by an altogether unforeseen development, of which the less said the better until the proper time. The foresight and imagination of a Raffles are obviously apt to outstrip his spoken words; but even in the course of speech his ideas would crystallise, quite palpably to the listener, and the sentence that began by throwing out a shadowy idea would culminate in a definite project, as the image comes into focus under the lens, and with as much detail into the bargain.

Suffice it that after a long night of it at the Albany, and but a bath and a cup of tea at my own flat, I found Raffles waiting for me in Piccadilly, and down we went together to the jaws of Jermyn Street. There we nodded, and I was proceeding down the hill when I turned on my heel as though I had forgotten something, and entered Jermyn Street not fifty yards behind Raffles. I had no thought of catching him up. But it so happened that I was in his wake in time to witness a first *contretemps* which did not amount to much at the time; this was merely the violent exit of another of Dan Levy's early callers into the very arms of Raffles. There was a heated apology, accepted with courteous composure, and followed by an excited outpouring which I did not come near enough to overhear. It was delivered by a little man in an aureole of indigo hair, who brushed his great sombrero violently as he spoke and Raffles listened. I could see from their manner that the collision which had just occurred was not the subject under discussion; but I failed to distinguish a word, though I listened outside a hatter's until Raffles had gone in and his new acquaintance had passed me with blazing eyes and a volley of husky vows in broken English.

"Another of Mr. Shylock's victims," thought I; and indeed he might have been bleeding internally from the loss of his pound of flesh; at any rate there was bloodshed in his eyes.

I stood a long time outside that hatter's window, and finally went in to choose a cap. But the light is wicked in those narrow shops, and this necessitated my carrying several caps to the broad daylight of the threshold to gauge their shades, and incidentally to achieve a swift survey of the street. Then they crowned me with an ingenious apparatus like a typewriter, to get the exact shape and measure of my skull, for I had intimated that I had no desire to dress it anywhere else for the future. All this must have taken up the most of twenty minutes, yet after getting as far as Mr. Shylock's I remembered that I required what one's hatter (and no one else) calls a "boater," and back I went to order one in addition to the cap. And as the next tack fetches the buoy, so my next perambulation (in which, however, I was thinking seriously of a new bowler) brought me face to face with Raffles once more.

We shouted and shook hands; our encounter had taken place almost under the money-lender's windows, and it was so un-English in its cordiality that between our slaps and grasps Raffles managed deftly to insert a stout packet in my breast pocket. I cannot think the most critical pedestrian could have seen it done. But streets have as many eyes as Argus, and some of them are always on one.

"They had to send to the bank for it," whispered Raffles. "It barely passed through their hands. But don't you let Shylock spot his own envelope!"

In another second he was saying something very different that anybody might have heard, and in yet another he was hustling me across Shylock's threshold. "I'll take you up and introduce you," he cried aloud. "You couldn't come to a better man, my dear fellow—he's the only honest one in Europe. Is Mr. Levy disengaged?"

A stunted young gentleman, who spoke as though he had a hare-lip or was in liquor, neither calamity having really befallen him, said that he thought so, but would see, which proceeded to do through a telephone, after shifting the indicator from "Through" to "Private." He slid off his stool at once, and another youth, of similar appearance and still more similar peculiarity of speech, who entered in a hurry at that moment, was told to hold on while he showed the gentlemen up-stairs. There were other clerks behind the mahogany bulwark, and we heard the newcomer greeting them hoarsely as we climbed up into the presence.

Dan Levy, as I must try to call him when Raffles is not varnishing my tale, looked a very big man at his enormous desk, but by no means so elephantine as at the tiny table in the Savoy Restaurant a month earlier. His privations had not only reduced his bulk to the naked eye, but made him look ten years younger. He wore the habiliments of a gentleman; even as he sat at his desk his well-cut coat and well-tied tie filled me with that inconsequent respect which the silk pyjamas had engendered in Raffles. But the great face that greeted us with a shrewd and rather scornful geniality impressed me yet more powerfully. In its massive features and its craggy contour it displayed the frank pugnacity of the pugilist rather than the low cunning of the traditional usurer; and the nose in particular, while of far healthier appearance than when I had seen it first and last, was both dominant and menacing in its immensity. It was a comfort to turn from this formidable countenance to that of Raffles, who had entered with his own serene unconscious confidence, and now introduced us with that inimitable air of light-hearted authority which stamped him in all shades of society.

"'Appy to meet you, sir. I hope you're well?" said Mr. Levy, dropping one aspirate but putting in the next with care. "Take a seat, sir, please."

But I kept my legs, though I felt them near to trembling, and, diving a hand into a breast pocket, I began working the contents out of the envelope that Raffles had given me, while I spoke out in a tone sufficiently rehearsed at the Albany overnight.

"I'm not so sure about the happiness," said I. "I mean about its lasting, Mr. Levy. I come from my friend, Mr. Edward Garland."

"I thought you came to borrow money!" interposed Raffles with much indignation. The moneylender was watching me with bright eyes and lips I could no longer see.

"I never said so," I rapped out at Raffles; and I thought I saw approval and encouragement behind his stare like truth at the bottom of the well.

"Who *is* the little biter?" the money-lender inquired of him with delightful insolence.

"An old friend of mine," replied Raffles, in an injured tone that made a convincing end of the old friendship. "I thought he was hard up, or I never should have brought him in to introduce to you."

"I didn't ask you for your introduction, Raffles," said I offensively. "I simply met you coming out as I was coming in. I thought you damned officious, if you ask me!"

Whereupon, with an Anglo-Saxon threat of subsequent violence to my person, Raffles flung open the door to leave us to our interview. This was exactly as it had been rehearsed. But Dan Levy called Raffles back. And that was exactly as we had hoped.

"Gentlemen, gentlemen!" said the Jew. "Please don't make a cockpit of my office, gentlemen; and pray, Mr. Raffles, don't leave me to the mercies of your very dangerous friend."

"You can be two to one if you like," I gasped valiantly. "*I* don't care."

And my chest heaved in accordance with my stage instructions, as also with a realism to which it was a relief to give full play.

"Come now," said Levy. "What did Mr. Garland send you about?"

"You know well enough," said I: "his debt to you."

"Don't be rude about it," said Levy. "What about the debt?"

"It's a damned disgrace!" said I.

"I quite agree," he chuckled. "It ought to 'ave been settled months ago."

"Months ago?" I echoed. "It's only twelve months since he borrowed three hundred pounds from you, and now you're sticking him for seven!"

"I am," said Levy, opening uncompromising lips that entirely disappeared again next instant.

"He borrows three hundred for a year at the outside, and you blackmail him for eight hundred when the year's up."

"You said 'seven' just now," interrupted Raffles, but in the voice of a man who was getting a fright.

"You also said 'blackmailing,'" added Dan Levy portentously. "Do you want to be thrown downstairs?"

"Do *you* deny the figures?" I retorted.

"No, I don't; have you got his repayment cards?"

"Yes, here in my hands, and they shan't leave them. You see, you're not aware," I added severely, as I turned to Raffles, "that this young fellow has already paid up one hundred in instalments; that's what makes the eight; and all this is what'll happen to you if you've been fool enough to get into the same boat."

The money-lender had borne with me longer than either of us had expected that he would; but now he wheeled back his chair and stood up, a pillar of peril and a mouthful of oaths.

"Is that all you've come to say?" he thundered. "If so, you young devil, out you go!"

"No, it isn't," said I, spreading out a document attached to the cards of receipt which Raffles had obtained from Teddy Garland; these I had managed to extract without anything else from the inner pocket in which I had been trying to empty out Raffles's envelope. "Here," I continued, "is a letter, written only yesterday, by you to Mr. Garland, in which you say, among other very insolent things: 'This is final, and absolutely no excuses of any kind will be tolerated or accepted. You have given ten times more trouble than your custom is worth, and I shall be glad to get rid of you. So you had better pay up before twelve o'clock to-morrow, as you may depend that the above threats will be carried out to the very letter, and steps will be taken to carry them into effect at that hour. This is your dead and last chance, and the last time I will write you on the subject.'"

"So it is," said Levy with an oath. "This is a very bad case, Mr. Raffles."

"I agree," said I. "And may I ask if you propose to 'get rid' of Mr. Garland by making him 'pay up' in full?"

"Before twelve o'clock to-day," said Dan Levy, with a snap of his prize-fighting jaws.

"Eight hundred, first and last, for the three hundred he borrowed a year ago?"

"That's it."

"Surely that's very hard on the boy," I said, reaching the conciliatory stage by degrees on which Raffles paid me many compliments later; but at the time he remarked, "I should say it was his own fault."

"Of course it is, Mr. Raffles," cried the moneylender, taking a more conciliatory tone himself. "It was my money; it was my three 'undred golden sovereigns; and you can sell what's yours for what it'll fetch, can't you?"

"Obviously," said Raffles.

"Very well, then, money's like anything else; if you haven't got it, and can't beg or earn it, you've got to buy it at a price. I sell my money, that's all. And I've a right to sell it at a fancy price if I can get a fancy price for it. A man may be a fool to pay my figure; that depends 'ow much he wants the money at the time, and it's his affair, not mine. Your gay young friend was all right if he hadn't defaulted, but a defaulter deserves to pay through the nose, and be damned to him. It wasn't me let your friend in; he let in himself, with his eyes open. Mr. Garland knew very well what I was charging him, and what I shouldn't 'esitate to charge over and above if he gave me half a chance. Why should I? Wasn't it in the bond? What do you all think I run my show for? It's business, Mr. Raffles, not robbery, my dear sir. All business is robbery, if you come to that. But you'll find mine is all above-board and in the bond."

"A very admirable exposition," said Raffles weightily.

"Not that it applies to you, Mr. Raffles," the other was adroit enough to add. "Mr. Garland was no friend of mine, and he was a fool, whereas I hope I may say that you're the one and not the other."

"Then it comes to this," said I, "that you mean him to pay up in full this morning?"

"By noon, and it's just gone ten."

"The whole seven hundred pounds?"

"Sterling," said Mr. Levy "No cheques entertained."

"Then," said I, with an air of final defeat, "there's nothing for it but to follow my instructions and pay you now on the nail!"

I did not look at Levy, but I heard the sudden intake of his breath at the sight of my bank-notes, and I felt its baleful exhalation on my forehead as I stooped and began counting them out upon his desk. I had made some progress before he addressed me in terms of protest. There was almost a tremor in his voice. I had no call to be so hasty; it looked as though I had been playing a game with him. Why couldn't I tell him I had the money with me all the time? The question was asked with a sudden oath, because I had gone on counting it out regardless of his overtures. I took as little notice of his anger.

"And now, Mr. Levy," I concluded, "may I ask you to return me Mr. Garland's promissory note?"

"Yes, you may ask and you shall receive!" he snarled, and opened his safe so violently that the keys fell out. Raffles replaced them with exemplary promptitude while the note of hand was being found.

The evil little document was in my possession at last. Levy roared down the tube, and the young man of the imperfect diction duly appeared.

"Take that young biter," cried Levy, "and throw him into the street. Call up Moses to lend you a 'and."

But the first murderer stood nonplussed, looking from Raffles to me, and finally inquiring which biter his master meant.

"That one!" bellowed the money-lender, shaking a lethal fist at me. "Mr. Raffles is a friend o' mine."

"But 'e'th a friend of 'ith too," lisped the young man. "Thimeon Markth come acroth the thtreet to tell me tho. He thaw them thake handth outthide our plathe, after he'd theen 'em arm-in-arm in Piccadilly, 'an he come in to thay tho in cathe—"

But the youth of limited articulation was not allowed to finish his explanation; he was grasped by the scruff of the neck and kicked and shaken out of the room, and his collar flung after him. I heard him blubbering on the stairs as Levy locked the door and put the key in his pocket. But I did not hear Raffles slip into the swivel chair behind the desk, or know that he had done so until the usurer and I turned round together.

"Out of that!" blustered Levy.

But Raffles tilted the chair back on its spring and laughed softly in his face.

"Not if I know it," said he. "If you don't open the door in about one minute I shall require this telephone of yours to ring up the police."

"The police, eh?" said Levy, with a sinister recovery of self-control. "You'd better leave that to me, you precious pair of swindlers!"

"Besides," continued Raffles, "of course you keep an *argumentum ad hominem* in one of these drawers. Ah, here it is, and just as well in my hands as in yours!"

He had opened the top drawer in the right-hand pedestal, and taken therefrom a big bulldog revolver; it was the work of few moments to empty its five chambers, and hand the pistol by its barrel to the owner.

"Curse you!" hissed the latter, hurling it into the fender with a fearful clatter. "But you'll pay for this, my fine gentlemen; this isn't sharp practice, but criminal fraud."

"The burden of proof," said Raffles, "lies with you. Meanwhile, will you be good enough to open that door instead of looking as sick as a cold mud-poultice?"

The money-lender had, indeed, turned as grey as his hair; and his eyebrows, which were black and looked dyed, stood out like smears of ink. Nevertheless, the simile which Raffles had employed with his own unfortunate facility was more picturesque than discreet. I saw it set Mr. Shylock thinking. Luckily, the evil of the day was sufficient for it and him; but so far from complying, he set his back to the locked door and swore a sweet oath never to budge.

"Oh, very well!" resumed Raffles, and the receiver was at his ear without more ado. "Is that the Exchange? Give me nine-two-double-three Gerrard, will you?"

"It's fraud," reiterated Levy. "And you know it."

"It's nothing of the sort, and *you* know it," murmured Raffles, with the proper pre-occupation of the man at the telephone.

"You lent the money," I added. "That's your business. It's nothing to do with you what he chooses to do with it."

"He's a cursed swindler," hissed Levy. "And you're his damned decoy!"

I was not sorry to see Raffles's face light up across the desk.

"Is that Howson, Anstruther and Martin?—they're only my solicitors, Mr. Levy. . . Put me through to Mr. Martin, please. . . That you, Charlie? . . . You might come in a cab to Jermyn Street—I forget the number—Dan Levy's, the money-lender's—thanks, old chap! . . . Wait a bit, Charlie—a constable. . ."

But Dan Levy had unlocked his door and flung it open.

"There you are, you scoundrels! But we'll meet again, my fine swell-mobsmen!"

Raffles was frowning at the telephone.

"I've been cut off," said he. "Wait a bit! Clear call for you, Mr. Levy, I believe!"

And they changed places, without exchanging another word until Raffles and I were on the stairs.

"Why, the 'phone's not even *through!*" yelled the money-lender, rushing out.

"But *we* are, Mr. Levy!" cried Raffles. And down we ran into the street.

V

THIN AIR

Raffles hailed a passing hansom, and had bundled me in before I realised that he was not coming with me.

"Drive down to the club for Teddy's cricket-bag," said he; "we'll make him get straight into flannels to save time. Order breakfast for three in half-an-hour precisely, and I'll tell him everything before you're back."

His eyes were shining with the prospect as I drove away, not sorry to escape the scene of that young man's awakening to better fortune than he deserved. For in my heart I could not quite forgive the act in which Raffles and I had caught him overnight. Raffles might make as light of it as he pleased; it was impossible for another to take his affectionately lenient view, not of the moral question involved, but of the breach of faith between friend and friend. My own feeling in the matter, however, if a little jaundiced, was not so strong as to prevent me from gloating over the victory in which I had just assisted. I thought of the notorious extortioner who had fallen to our unscrupulous but not indictable wiles; and my heart tinkled with the hansom bell. I thought of the good that we had done for once, of the undoubted wrong we had contrived to right by a species of justifiable chicanery. And I forgot all about the youth whose battle we had fought and won, until I found myself ordering his breakfast, and having his cricket-bag taken out to my cab.

Raffles was waiting for me in the Albany courtyard. I thought he was frowning at the sky, which was not what it had been earlier in the morning, until I remembered how little time there was to lose.

"Haven't you seen anything of him?" he cried as I jumped out.

"Of whom, Raffles?"

"Teddy, of course!"

"Teddy Garland? Has he gone out?"

"Before I got in," said Raffles, grimly. "I wonder where the devil he is!"

He had paid the cabman and taken down the bag himself. I followed him up to his rooms.

"But what's the meaning of it, Raffles?"

"That's what I want to know."

"Could he have gone out for a paper?"

"They were all here before I went. I left them on his bed."

"Or for a shave?"

"That's more likely; but he's been out nearly an hour."

"But you can't have been gone much longer yourself, Raffles, and I understood you left him fast asleep?"

"That's the worst of it, Bunny. He must have been shamming. Barraclough saw him go out ten minutes after me."

"Could you have disturbed him when you went?"

Raffles shook his head.

"I never shut a door more carefully in my life. I made row enough when I came back, Bunny, on purpose to wake him up, and I can tell you it gave me a turn when there wasn't a sound from in there! He'd shut all the doors after him; it was a second or two before I had the pluck to open them. I thought something horrible had happened!"

"You don't think so still?"

"I don't know what to think," said Raffles, gloomily; "nothing has panned out as I thought it would. You must remember that we have given ourselves away to Dan Levy, whatever else we have done, and without doubt set up the enemy of our lives in the very next street. It's close quarters, Bunny; we shall have an expert eye upon us for some time to come. But I should rather enjoy that than otherwise, if only Teddy hadn't bolted in this rotten way."

Never had I known Raffles in so pessimistic a mood. I did not share his sombre view of either matter, though I confined my remarks to the one that seemed to weigh most heavily on his mind.

"A guinea to a gooseberry," I wagered, "that you find your man safe and sound at Lord's."

"I rang them up ten minutes ago," said Raffles. "They hadn't heard of him then; besides, here's his cricket-bag."

"He may have been at the club when I fetched it away—I never asked."

"I did, Bunny. I rang them up as well, just after you had left."

"Then what about his father's house?"

"That's our one chance," said Raffles. "They're not on the telephone, but now that you're here I've a good mind to drive out and see if Teddy's there. You know what a state he was in last night, and you know how a thing can seem worse when you wake and remember it than it did at the time it happened. I begin to hope he's gone straight to old Garland with the whole story; in that case he's bound to come back for his kit; and by Jove, Bunny, there's a step upon the stairs!"

We had left the doors open behind us, and a step it was, ascending hastily enough to our floor. But it was not the step of a very young man, and Raffles was the first to recognise the fact; his face fell as we looked at each other for a single moment of suspense; in another he was out of the room, and I heard him greeting Mr. Garland on the landing.

"Then you haven't brought Teddy with you?" I heard Raffles add.

"Do you mean to say he isn't here?" replied so pleasant a voice— in accents of such acute dismay—that Mr. Garland had my sympathy before we met.

"He has been," said Raffles, "and I'm expecting him back every minute. Won't you come in and wait, Mr. Garland?"

The pleasant voice made an exclamation of premature relief; the pair entered, and I was introduced to the last person I should have suspected of being a retired brewer at all, much less of squandering his money in retirement as suggested by his son. I was prepared for a conventional embodiment of reckless prosperity, for a pseudo-military type in louder purple and finer linen than the real thing. I shook hands instead with a gentle, elderly man, whose kindly eyes beamed bravely amid careworn furrows, and whose slightly diffident yet wholly cordial address won my heart outright.

"So you've lost no time in welcoming the wanderer!" said he. "You're nearly as bad as my boy, who was quite bent on seeing Raffles last night or first thing this morning. He told me he should stay the night in town if necessary, and he evidently has."

There was still a trace of anxiety in the father's manner, but there was also a twinkle in his eyes, which kindled with genial fires as Raffles gave a perfectly truthful account of the young man's movements (as distinct from his words and deeds) overnight.

"And what do you think of his great news?" asked Mr. Garland. "Was it a surprise to you, Raffles?"

Raffles shook his head with a rather weary smile, and I sat up in my chair. What great news was this?

"This son of mine has just got engaged," explained Mr. Garland for my benefit. "And as a matter of fact it's his engagement that brings me here; you gentlemen mustn't think I want to keep an eagle eye upon him; but Miss Belsize has just wired to say she is coming up early to go with us to the match, instead of meeting at Lord's, and I thought she would be so disappointed not to find Teddy, especially as they are bound to see very little of each other all day."

I for my part was wondering why I had not heard of Miss Belsize or this engagement from Raffles. He must himself have heard of it last thing at night in the next room, while I was star-gazing here at the open window. Yet in all the small hours he had never told me of a circumstance which extenuated young Garland's conduct if it did nothing else. Even now it was not from Raffles that I received either word or look of explanation. But his face had suddenly lit up.

"May I ask," he exclaimed, "if the telegram was to Teddy or to you, Mr. Garland?"

"It was addressed to Teddy, but of course I opened it in his absence."

"Could it have been an answer to an invitation or suggestion of his?"

"Very easily. They had lunch together yesterday, and Camilla might have had to consult Lady Laura."

"Then that's the whole thing!" cried Raffles. "Teddy was on his way home while you were on yours into town! How did you come?"

"In the brougham."

"Through the Park?"

"Yes."

"While he was in a hansom in Knightsbridge or Kensington Gore! That's how you missed him," said Raffles confidently. "If you drive straight back you'll be in time to take him on to Lord's."

Mr. Garland begged us both to drive back with him; and we thought we might; we decided that we would, and were all three under way in about a minute. Yet it was considerably after eleven when we bowled through Kensington to a house that I had never seen before, a house since swept away by the flowing tide of flats, but I can still see every stone and slate of it as clearly as on that summer morning more than ten years ago. It stood just off the thoroughfare, in grounds of its own out of all keeping with their metropolitan environment; they ran from one side-street to another, and further back than we could see. Vivid lawn and towering tree, brilliant beds and crystal vineries, struck one more forcibly (and favourably) than the mullioned and turreted mansion of a house. And yet a double stream of omnibuses rattled incessantly within a few yards of the steps on which the three of us soon stood nonplussed.

Mr. Edward had not been seen or heard of at the house. Neither had Miss Belsize arrived; that was the one consolatory feature.

"Come into the library," said Mr. Garland; and when we were among his books, which were somewhat beautifully bound and cased in glass, he turned to Raffles and added hoarsely: "There's something in all this I haven't been told, and I insist on knowing what it is."

"But you know as much as I do," protested Raffles. "I went out leaving Teddy asleep and came back to find him flown."

"What time was that?"

"Between nine and half-past when I went out. I was away nearly an hour."

"Why leave him asleep at that time of morning?"

"I wanted him to have every minute he could get. We had been sitting up rather late."

"But why, Raffles? What could you have to talk about all night when you were tired and it was Teddy's business to keep fresh for to-day? Why, after all, should he want to see you the moment you got back? He's not the first young fellow who's got rather suddenly engaged to a charming girl; is he in any trouble about it, Raffles?"

"About his engagement—not that I'm aware."

"Then he is in some trouble?"

"He was, Mr. Garland," answered Raffles. "I give you my word that he isn't now."

Mr. Garland grasped the back of a chair.

"Was it some money trouble, Raffles? Of course, if my boy has given you his confidence, I have no right simply as his father—"

"It is hardly that, sir," said Raffles, gently; "it is I who have no right to give him away. But if you don't mind leaving it at that, Mr. Garland, there is perhaps no harm in my saying that it *was* about some little temporary embarrassment that Teddy was so anxious to see me."

"And you helped him?" cried the poor man, plainly torn between gratitude and humiliation.

"Not out of my pocket," replied Raffles, smiling. "The matter was not so serious as Teddy thought; it only required adjustment."

"God bless you, Raffles!" murmured Mr. Garland, with a catch in his voice. "I won't ask for a single detail. My poor boy went to the right man; he knew better than to come to me. Like father, like son!" he muttered to himself, and dropped into the chair he had been handling, and bent his head over his folded arms.

He seemed to have forgotten the untoward effect of Teddy's disappearance in the peculiar humiliation of its first cause. Raffles took

E.W. HORNUNG

out his watch, and held up the dial for me to see. It was after the half-hour now; but at this moment a servant entered with a missive, and the master recovered his self-control.

"This'll be from Teddy!" he cried, fumbling with his glasses. "No; it's for him, and by special messenger. I'd better open it. I don't suppose it's Miss Belsize again."

"Miss Belsize is in the drawing-room, sir," said the man. "She said you were not to be disturbed."

"Oh, tell her we shan't be long," said Mr. Garland, with a new strain of trouble in his tone. "Listen to this—listen to this," he went on before the door was shut: "'What has happened? Lost toss. Whipham plays if you don't turn up in time.—J. S.'"

"Jack Studley," said Raffles, "the Cambridge skipper."

"I know! I know! And Whipham's reserve man, isn't he?"

"And another wicket-keeper, worse luck!" exclaimed Raffles. "If he turns out and takes a single ball, and Teddy is only one over late, it will still be too late for him to play."

"Then it's too late already," said Mr. Garland, sinking back into his chair with a groan.

"But that note from Studley may have been half-an-hour on the way."

"No, Raffles, it's not an ordinary note; it's a message telephoned straight from Lord's—probably within the last few minutes—to a messenger office not a hundred yards from this door!"

Mr. Garland sat staring miserably at the carpet; he was beginning to look ill with perplexity and suspense. Raffles himself, who had turned his back upon us with a shrug of acquiescence in the inevitable, was a monument of discomfiture as he stood gazing through a glass door into the adjoining conservatory. There was no actual window in the library, but this door was a single sheet of plate-glass into which a man might well have walked, and I can still see Raffles in full-length silhouette upon a panel of palms and tree-ferns. I see the silhouette grow tall and straight again before my eyes, the door open, and Raffles listening with an alert lift of the head. I, too, hear something, an elfin hiss, a fairy fusillade, and then the sudden laugh with which Raffles rejoined us in the body of the room.

"It's raining!" he cried, waving a hand above his head. "Have you a barometer, Mr. Garland?"

"That's an aneroid under the lamp-bracket."

"How often do you set the indicator?"

"Last thing every night. I remember it was between Fair and Change when I went to bed. It made me anxious."

"It may make you thankful now. It's between Change and Rain this morning. And the rain's begun, and while there's rain there's hope!"

In a twinkling Raffles had regained all his own irresistible buoyancy and assurance. But the older man was not capable of so prompt a recovery.

"Something has happened to my boy!"

"But not necessarily anything terrible."

"If I knew what, Raffles—if only I knew what!"

Raffles eyed the pale and twitching face with sidelong solicitude. He himself had the confident expression which always gave me confidence; the rattle on the conservatory roof was growing louder every minute.

"I intend to find out," said he; "and if the rain goes on long enough, we may still see Teddy playing when it stops. But I shall want your help, sir."

"I am ready to go with you anywhere, Raffles."

"You can only help me, Mr. Garland, by staying where you are."

"Where I am?"

"In the house all day," said Raffles firmly. "It is absolutely essential to my idea."

"And that is, Raffles?"

"To save Teddy's face, in the first instance. I shall drive straight up to Lord's, in your brougham if I may. I know Studley rather well; he shall keep Teddy's place open till the last possible moment."

"But how shall you account for his absence?" I asked.

"I shall account for it all right," said Raffles darkly. "I can save his face for the time being, at all events at Lord's."

"But that's the only place that matters," said I.

"On the contrary, Bunny, this very house matters even more as long as Miss Belsize is here. You forget that they're engaged, and that she's in the next room now."

"Good God!" whispered Mr. Garland. "I had forgotten that myself."

"She is the last who must know of this affair," said Raffles, with, I thought, undue authority. "And you are the only one who can keep it from her, sir."

"I?"

"Miss Belsize mustn't go up to Lord's this morning. She would only spoil her things, and you may tell her from me that there would be no play for an hour after this, even if it stopped this minute, which it won't. Meanwhile let her think that Teddy's weatherbound with the rest of them in the pavilion; but she mustn't come until you hear from me again; and the best way to keep her here is to stay with her yourself."

"And when may I expect to hear?" asked Mr. Garland as Raffles held out his hand.

"Let me see. I shall be at Lord's in less than twenty minutes; another five or ten should polish off Studley; and then I shall barricade myself in the telephone-box and ring up every hospital in town! You see, it may be an accident after all, though I don't think so. You won't hear from me on the point unless it is; the fewer messengers flying about the better, if you agree with me as to the wisdom of keeping the matter dark at this end."

"Oh, yes, I agree with you, Raffles; but it will be a terribly hard task for me!"

"It will, indeed, Mr. Garland. Yet no news is always good news, and I promise to come straight to you the moment I have news of any kind."

With that they shook hands, our host with an obvious reluctance that turned to a less understandable dismay as I also prepared to take my leave of him.

"What!" cried he, "am I to be left quite alone to hoodwink that poor girl and hide my own anxiety?"

"There's no reason why you should come, Bunny," said Raffles to me. "If either of them is a one-man job, it's mine."

Our host said no more, but he looked at me so wistfully that I could not but offer to stay with him if he wished it; and when at length the drawing-room door had closed upon him and his son's *fiancee*, I took an umbrella from the stand and saw Raffles through the providential downpour into the brougham.

"I'm sorry, Bunny," he muttered between the butler in the porch and the coachman on the box. "This sort of thing is neither in my line nor yours, but it serves us right for straying from the path of candid crime. We should have opened a safe for that seven hundred."

"But what do you really think is at the bottom of this extraordinary disappearance?"

"Some madness or other, I'm afraid; but if that boy is still in the land of the living, I shall have him before the sun goes down on his insanity."

"And what about this engagement of his?" I pursued. "Do you disapprove of it?"

"Why on earth should I?" asked Raffles, rather sharply, as he plunged from under my umbrella into the brougham.

"Because you never told me when he told you," I replied. "Is the girl beneath him?"

Raffles looked at me inscrutably with his clear blue eyes.

"You'd better find out for yourself," said he. "Tell the coachman to hurry up to Lord's—and pray that this rain may last!"

E.W. HORNUNG

VI

Camilla Belsize

It would be hard to find a better refuge on a rainy day than the amphibious retreat described by Raffles as a "country house in Kensington." There was a good square hall, full of the club comforts so welcome in a home, such as magazines and cigarettes, and a fire when the rain set in. The usual rooms opened off the hall, and the library was not the only one that led on into the conservatory; the drawing-room was another, in which I heard voices as I lit a cigarette among the palms and tree-ferns. It struck me that poor Mr. Garland was finding it hard work to propitiate the lady whom Raffles had deemed unworthy of mention overnight. But I own I was in no hurry to take over the invidious task. To me it need prove nothing more; to him, anguish; but I could not help feeling that even as matters stood I was quite sufficiently embroiled in these people's affairs. Their name had been little more than a name to me until the last few hours. Only yesterday I might have hesitated to nod to Teddy Garland at the club, so seldom had we met. Yet here was I helping Raffles to keep the worst about the son from the father's knowledge, and on the point of helping that father to keep what might easily prove worse still from his daughter-in-law to be. And all the time there was the worst of all to be hidden from everybody concerning Raffles and me!

Meanwhile I explored a system of flower-houses and vineries that ran out from the conservatory in a continuous chain—each link with its own temperature and its individual scent—and not a pane but rattled and streamed beneath the timely torrent. It was in a fernery where a playing fountain added its tuneful drop to the noisy deluge that the voices of the drawing-room sounded suddenly at my elbow, and I was introduced to Miss Belsize before I could recover from my surprise. My foolish face must have made her smile in spite of herself, for I did not see quite the same smile again all day; but it made me her admirer on the spot, and I really think she warmed to me for amusing her even for a moment.

So we began rather well; and that was a mercy in the light of poor Mr. Garland's cynically prompt departure; but we did not go on quite as well as we had begun. I do not say that Miss Belsize was in a bad temper, but emphatically she was not pleased, and I for one had the utmost sympathy with her displeasure. She was simply but exquisitely dressed, with unostentatious touches of Cambridge blue and a picture hat that really was a picture. Yet on a perfect stranger in a humid rockery she was wasting what had been meant for mankind at Lord's. The only consolation I could suggest was that by this time Lord's would be more humid still.

"And so there's something to be said for being bored to tears under shelter, Miss Belsize." Miss Belsize did not deny that she was bored.

"But there's plenty of shelter there," said she.

"Packed with draggled dresses and squelching shoes! You might swim for it before they admitted you to that Pavilion, you know."

"But if the ground's under water, how can they play to-day?"

"They can't, Miss Belsize, I don't mind betting."

That was a rash remark.

"Then why doesn't Teddy come back?"

"Oh, well, you know," I hedged, "you can never be quite absolutely sure. It might clear up. They're bound to give it a chance until the afternoon. And the players can't leave till stumps are drawn."

"I should have thought Teddy could have come home to lunch," said Miss Belsize, "even if he had to go back afterwards."

"I shouldn't wonder if he did come," said I, conceiving the bare possibility: "and A.J. with him."

"Do you mean Mr. Raffles?"

"Yes, Miss Belsize; he's the only A.J. that counts!"

Camilla Belsize turned slightly in the basket-chair to which she had confided her delicate frock, and our eyes met almost for the first time. Certainly we had not exchanged so long a look before, for she had been watching the torpid goldfish in the rockery pool, and I admiring her bold profile and the querulous poise of a fine head as I tried to argue her out of all desire for Lord's. Suddenly our eyes met, as I say, and hers dazzled me; they were soft and yet brilliant, tender and yet cynical, calmly reckless, audaciously sentimental—all that and more as I see them now on looking back; but at the time I was merely dazzled.

"So you and Mr. Raffles are great friends?" said Miss Belsize, harking back to a remark of Mr. Garland's in introducing us.

"Rather!" I replied.

"Are you as great a friend of his as Teddy is?"

I liked that, but simply said I was an older friend. "Raffles and I were at school together," I added loftily.

"Really? I should have thought he was before your time."

"No, only senior to me. I happened to be his fag."

"And what sort of a schoolboy was Mr. Raffles?" inquired Miss Belsize, not by any means in the tone of a devotee. But I reflected that her own devotion was bespoke, and not improbably tainted with some little jealousy of Raffles.

"He was the most Admirable Crichton who was ever at the school," said I: "captain of the eleven, the fastest man in the fifteen, athletic champion, and an ornament of the Upper Sixth."

"And you worshipped him, I suppose?"

"Absolutely."

My companion had been taking renewed interest in the goldfish; now she looked at me again with the cynical light full on in her eyes.

"You must be rather disappointed in him now!"

"Disappointed! Why?" I asked with much outward amusement. But I was beginning to feel uncomfortable.

"Of course I don't know much about him," remarked Miss Belsize as though she cared less.

"But does anybody know anything of Mr. Raffles except as a cricketer?"

"I do," said I, with injudicious alacrity.

"Well," said Miss Belsize, "what else is he?"

"The best fellow in the world, among other things."

"But what other things?"

"Ask Teddy!" I said unluckily.

"I have," replied Miss Belsize. "But Teddy doesn't know. He often wonders how Mr. Raffles can afford to play so much cricket without doing any work."

"Does he, indeed!"

"Many people do."

"And what do they say about him?"

Miss Belsize hesitated, watching me for a moment and the goldfish rather longer. The rain sounded louder, and the fountain as though it had been turned on again, before she answered:

"More than their prayers, no doubt!"

"Do you mean," I almost gasped, "as to the way Raffles gets his living?"

"Yes."

"You might tell me the kind of things they say, Miss Belsize!"

"But if there's no truth in them?"

"I'll soon tell you if there is or not."

"But suppose I don't care either way?" said Miss Belsize with a brilliant smile.

"Then I care so much that I should be extremely grateful to you."

"Mind, I don't believe it myself, Mr. Manders."

"You don't believe—"

"That Mr. Raffles lives by his wits and—his cricket!"

I jumped to my feet.

"Is that all they say about him?" I cried.

"Isn't it enough?" asked Miss Belsize, astonished in her turn at my demeanour.

"Oh, quite enough, quite enough!" said I. "It's only the most scandalously unfair and utterly untrue report that ever got about— that's all!"

This heavy irony was, of course, intended to convey the impression that one's first explosion of relief had been equally ironical. But I was to discover that Camilla Belsize was never easily deceived; it was unpleasantly apparent in her bold eyes before she opened her firm mouth.

"Yet you seemed to expect something worse," she said at length.

"What could be worse?" I asked, my back against the wall of my own indiscretion. "Why, a man like A.J. Raffles would rather be any mortal thing than a paid amateur!"

"But you haven't told me what he *is*, Mr. Manders."

"And you haven't told me, Miss Belsize, why you're so interested in A. J. after all!" I retorted, getting home for once, and sitting down again on the strength of it.

But Miss Belsize was my superior to the last; in the single moment of my ascendency she made me blush for it and for myself. She would be quite frank with me: my friend Mr. Raffles did interest her rather more than she cared to say. It was because Teddy thought so much of him, that was the only reason, and her one excuse for all inquisitive questions and censorious remarks. I must have thought her very rude; but now I knew. Mr. Raffles had been such a friend to Teddy; sometimes she wondered whether he was quite a good friend; and there I had "the whole thing in a nutshell."

I had indeed! And I knew the nut, and had tasted its bitter kernel too often to make any mistake about it. Jealousy was its other name. But I did not care how jealous Miss Belsize became of Raffles as long as jealousy did not beget suspicion; and my mind was not entirely relieved on that point.

We dropped the whole subject, however, with some abruptness; and the rest of our conversation in the rockery, and in the steaming orchid-house and further vineries which we proceeded to explore together, was quite refreshingly tame. Yet I think it was on this desultory tour, to the still incessant accompaniment of rain on the glasshouses, that Camilla's mother took shape in my mind as the Lady Laura Belsize, an apparently impecunious widow reduced to "semi-detachment down the river" and suburban neighbours whose manners and customs my companion hit off with vivacious intolerance. She told me how she had shocked them by smoking cigarettes in the back garden, and pronounced a gratuitous conviction that I of all people would have been no less scandalised! That was in the uttermost vinery, and in another minute two Sullivans were in full blast under the vines. I remember discovering that the great brand was not unfamiliar to Miss Belsize, and even gathering that it was Raffles himself who had made it known to her. Raffles, whom she did not "know much about," or consider "quite a good friend" for Teddy Garland!

I was becoming curious to see this antagonistic pair together; but it was the middle of the afternoon before Raffles reappeared, though Mr. Garland told me he had received an optimistic note from him by special messenger earlier in the day. I felt I might have been told a little more, considering the intimate part I was already playing as a stranger in a strange house. But I was only too thankful to find that Raffles had so far infected our host with his confidence as to tide us through luncheon with far fewer embarrassments than before; nor did Mr. Garland desert us again until the butler with a visitor's card brought about his abrupt departure from the conservatory.

Then my troubles began afresh. It stopped raining at last; if Miss Belsize could have had her way we should all have started for Lord's that minute. I took her into the garden to show her the state of the lawns, coldly scintillant with standing water and rimmed by regular canals. Lord's would be like them, only fifty times worse; play had no doubt been abandoned on that quagmire for the day. Miss Belsize was not so sure about that; why should we not drive over and find out? I said that was the surest way of missing Teddy. She said a hansom would take us there and back in a half-an-hour. I gained time disputing that statement, but said if we went at all I was sure Mr. Garland would want to go with us, and that in his own brougham. All this on the crown of a sloppy path, and when Miss Belsize asked me how many more times I was going to change my ground, I could not help looking at her absurd shoes sinking into the softened gravel, and saying I thought it was for her to do that. Miss Belsize took my advice to the extent of turning upon a submerged heel, though with none too complimentary a smile; and then it was that I saw what I had been curious to see all day. Raffles was coming down the path towards us. And I saw Miss Belsize hesitate and stiffen before shaking hands with him.

"They've given it up as a bad job at last," said he. "I've just come from Lord's, and Teddy won't be very long."

"Why didn't you bring him with you?" asked Miss Belsize pertinently.

"Well, I thought you ought to know the worst at once," said Raffles, rather lamely for him; "and then a man playing in a 'Varsity match is never quite his own master, you know. Still, he oughtn't to keep you waiting much longer."

It was perhaps unfortunately put; at any rate Miss Belsize took it pretty plainly amiss, and I saw her colour rise as she declared she had been waiting in the hope of seeing some cricket. Since that was at an end she must be thinking of getting home, and would just say good-bye to Mr. Garland. This sudden decision took me as much by surprise as I believe it took Miss Belsize herself; but having announced her intention, however hot-headedly, she proceeded to action by way of the conservatory and the library door, while Raffles and I went through into the hall the other way.

"I'm afraid I've put my foot in it," said he to me. "But it's just as well, since I needn't tell you there's no sign of Teddy up at Lord's."

"Have you been there all day?" I asked him under my breath.

"Except when I went to the office of this rag," replied Raffles, brandishing an evening paper that ill deserved his epithet. "See what they say about Teddy here."

And I held my breath while Raffles showed me a stupendous statement in the stop-press column: it was to the effect that E.M. Garland (Eton and Trinity) might be unable to keep wicket for Cambridge after all, "owing to the serious illness of his father."

E.W. HORNUNG

"His father!" I exclaimed. "Why, his father's closeted with somebody or other at this very moment behind the door you're looking at!"

"I know, Bunny. I've seen him."

"But what an extraordinary fabrication to get into a decent paper! I don't wonder you went to the office about it."

"You'll wonder still less when I tell you I have an old pal on the staff."

"Of course you made him take it straight out?"

"On the contrary, Bunny, I persuaded him to put it in!"

And Raffles chuckled in my face as I have known him chuckle over many a more felonious—but less incomprehensible—exploit.

"Didn't you see, Bunny, how bad the poor old boy looked in his library this morning? That gave me my idea; the fiction is at least founded on fact. I wonder you don't see the point; as a matter of fact, there are two points, just as there were two jobs I took on this morning; one was to find Teddy, and the other was to save his face at Lord's. Well, I haven't actually found him yet; but if he's in the land of the living he will see this statement, and when he does see it even you may guess what he will do! Meanwhile, there's nothing but sympathy for him at Lord's. Studley couldn't have been nicer; a place will be kept for Teddy up to the eleventh hour to-morrow. And if that isn't killing two birds with one stone, Bunny, may I never perform the feat!"

"But what will old Garland say, A. J.?"

"He has already said, Bunny. I told him what I was doing in a note before lunch, and the moment I arrived just now he came out to hear what I had done. He doesn't mind what I do so long as I find Teddy and save his face before the world at large and Miss Belsize in particular. Look out, Bunny—here she is!"

The excitement in his whisper was not characteristic of Raffles, but it was less remarkable than the change in Camilla Belsize as she entered the hall through the drawing-room as we had done before her. For one moment I suspected her of eavesdropping; then I saw that all traces of personal pique had vanished from her face, and that some anxiety for another had taken its place. She came up to Raffles and me as though she had forgiven both of us our trespasses of two or three minutes ago.

"I didn't go into the library after all," she said, looking askance at the library door. "I am afraid Mr. Garland is having a trying interview with somebody. I had just a glimpse of the man's face as I hesitated, and I thought I recognised him."

"Who was it?" I asked, for I myself had wondered who the rather mysterious visitor might be for whom Mr. Garland had deserted us so abruptly in the conservatory, and with whom he was still conferring in the hour of so many issues.

"I believe it's a dreadful man I know by sight down the river," said Miss Belsize; and hardly had she spoke before the library door opened and out came the dreadful man in the portentous person of Dan Levy, the usurer of European notoriety, our victim of the morning and our certain enemy for life.

VII

In Which We Fail to Score

M r. Levy sailed in with frock-coat flying, shiny hat in hand; he was evidently prepared for us, and Raffles for once behaved as though we were prepared for Mr. Levy. Of myself I cannot speak. I was ready for a terrific scene. But Raffles was magnificent, and to do our enemy justice he was quite as good; they faced each other with a nod and a smile of mutual suavity, shot with underlying animosity on the one side and delightful defiance on the other. Not a word was said or a tone employed to betray the true situation between the three of us; for I took my cue from the two protagonists just in time to preserve the triple truce. Meanwhile Mr. Garland, obviously distressed as he was, and really ill as he looked, was not the least successful of us in hiding his emotions; for having expressed a grim satisfaction in the coincidence of our all knowing each other, he added that he supposed Miss Belsize was an exception, and presented Mr. Levy forthwith as though he were an ordinary guest.

"You must find a better exception than this young lady!" cried that worthy with a certain *aplomb*. "I know you very well by sight, Miss Belsize, and your mother, Lady Laura, into the bargain."

"Really?" said Miss Belsize, without returning the compliment at her command.

"The bargain!" muttered Raffles to me with sly irony. The echo was not meant for Levy's ears, but it reached them nevertheless, and was taken up with adroit urbanity.

"I didn't mean to use a trade term," explained the Jew, "though bargains, I confess, are somewhat in my line; and I don't often get the worst of one, Mr. Raffles; when I do, the other fellow usually lives to repent it."

It was said with a laugh for the lady's benefit, but with a gleam of the eyes for ours. Raffles answered the laugh with a much heartier one; the look he ignored. I saw Miss Belsize beginning to watch the pair, and only interrupted by the arrival of the tea-tray, over which Mr. Garland begged her to preside. Mr. Garland seemed to have an anxious eye upon us all in turn; at Raffles he looked wistfully as though burning to get him to himself for further consultation; but the fact that he refrained from doing so, coupled with a grimly punctilious manner towards the money-lender, gave the impression that his son's whereabouts was no longer the sole anxiety.

"And yet," remarked Miss Belsize, as we formed a group about her in the firelight, "you seem to have met your match the other day, Mr. Levy?"

"Where was that, Miss Belsize?"

"Somewhere on the Continent, wasn't it? It got into the newspapers, I know, but I forget the name of the place."

"Do you mean when my wife and I were robbed at Carlsbad?"

I was holding my breath now as I had not held it all day. Raffles was merely smiling into his teacup as one who knew all about the affair.

"Carlsbad it was!" certified Miss Belsize, as though it mattered. "I remember now."

"I don't call that meeting your match," said the money-lender. "An unarmed man with a frightened wife at his elbow is no match for a desperate criminal with a loaded revolver."

"Was it as bad as all that?" whispered Camilla Belsize.

Up to this point one had felt her to be forcing the unlucky topic with the best of intentions towards us all; now she was interested in the episode for its own sake, and eager for more details than Mr. Levy had a mind to impart.

"It makes a good tale, I know," said he, "but I shall prefer telling it when they've got the man. If you want to know any more, Miss Belsize, you'd better ask Mr. Raffles; 'e was in our hotel, and came in for all the excitement. But it was just a trifle too exciting for me and my wife."

"Raffles at Carlsbad?" exclaimed Mr. Garland.

Miss Belsize only stared.

"Yes," said Raffles. "That's where I had the pleasure of meeting Mr. Levy."

"Didn't you know he was there?" inquired the money-lender of our host. And he looked sharply at Raffles as Mr. Garland replied that this was the first he had heard of it.

"But it's the first we've seen of each other, sir," said Raffles, "except those few minutes this morning. And I told you I only got back last night."

"But you never told me you had been at Carlsbad, Raffles!"

"It's a sore subject, you see," said Raffles, with a sigh and a laugh. "Isn't it, Mr. Levy?"

"You seem to find it so," replied the moneylender.

They were standing face to face in the firelight, each with a shoulder against the massive chimney-piece; and Camilla Belsize was still staring at them both from her place behind the tea-tray; and I was watching the three of them by turns from the other side of the hall.

"But you're the fittest man I know. Raffles," pursued old Garland with terrible tact. "What on earth were you doing at a place like Carlsbad?"

"The cure," said Raffles. "There's nothing else to do there—is there, Mr. Levy?"

Levy replied with his eyes on Raffles:

"Unless you've got to cope with a *swell mobsman* who steals your wife's jewels and then gets in such a funk that he practically gives them back again!"

The emphasised term was the one that Dan Levy had applied to Raffles and myself in his own office that very morning.

"Did he give them back again?" asked Camilla Belsize, breaking her silence on an eager note.

Raffles turned to her at once.

"The jewels were found buried in the woods," said he. "Out there everybody thought the thief had simply hidden them. But no doubt Mr. Levy has the better information."

Mr. Levy smiled sardonically in the firelight. And it was at this point I followed the example of Miss Belsize and put in my one belated word.

"I shouldn't have thought there was such a thing as a swell mob in the wilds of Austria," said I.

"There isn't," admitted the money-lender readily. "But your true mobsman knows his whole blooming Continent as well as Piccadilly Circus. His 'ead-quarters are in London, but a week's journey at an hour's notice is nothing to him if the swag looks worth it. Mrs. Levy's necklace was actually taken at Carlsbad, for instance, but the odds are that it was marked down at some London theatre—or restaurant, eh, Mr. Raffles?"

"I'm afraid I can't offer an expert opinion," said Raffles very merrily as their eyes met. "But if the man was an Englishman and knew that you were one, why didn't he bully you in the vulgar tongue?"

"Who told you he didn't?" cried Levy, with a sudden grin that left no doubt about the thought behind it. To me that thought had been obvious from its birth within the last few minutes; but this expression of it was as obvious a mistake.

"Who told me anything about it," retorted Raffles, "except yourself and Mrs. Levy? Your gospels clashed a little here and there; but both agreed that the fellow threatened you in German as well as with a revolver."

"We thought it was German," rejoined Levy, with dexterity. "It might 'ave been 'Industani or 'Eathen Chinee for all I know! But there was no error about the revolver. I can see it covering me, and his shooting eye looking along the barrel into mine—as plainly as I'm looking into yours now, Mr. Raffles."

Raffles laughed outright.

"I hope I'm a pleasanter spectacle, Mr. Levy? I remember your telling me that the other fellow looked the most colossal cut-throat."

"So he did," said Levy; "he looked a good deal worse than he need to have done. His face was blackened and disguised, but his teeth were as white as yours are."

"Any other little point in common?"

"I had a good look at the hand that pointed the revolver."

Raffles held out his hands.

"Better have a good look at mine."

"His were as black as his face, but even yours are no smoother or better kept."

"Well, I hope you'll clap the bracelets on them yet, Mr. Levy."

"You'll get your wish, I promise you, Mr. Raffles."

"You don't mean to say you've spotted your man?" cried A.J. airily.

"I've got my eye on him!" replied Dan Levy, looking Raffles through and through.

"And won't you tell us who he is?" asked Raffles, returning that deadly look with smiling interest, but answering a tone as deadly in one that maintained the note of persiflage in spite of Daniel Levy.

For Levy alone had changed the key with his last words; to that point I declare the whole passage might have gone for banter before the keenest eyes and the sharpest ears in Europe. I alone could know what a duel the two men were fighting behind their smiles. I alone could follow the finer shades, the mutual play of glance and gesture, the subtle tide of covert battle. So now I saw Levy debating with himself as to whether he should accept this impudent challenge and denounce Raffles there and then. I saw him hesitate, saw him reflect. The crafty, coarse, emphatic face was easily read; and when it suddenly lit up with a baleful light, I felt we might be on our guard against something more malign than mere reckless denunciation.

"Yes!" whispered a voice I hardly recognised. "Won't you tell us who it was?"

"Not yet," replied Levy, still looking Raffles full in the eyes. "But I know all about him now!"

I looked at Miss Belsize; she it was who had spoken, her pale face set, her pale lips trembling. I remembered her many questions about Raffles during the morning. And I began to wonder whether after all I was the only entirely understanding witness of what had passed here in the firelit hall.

Mr. Garland, at any rate, had no inkling of the truth. Yet even in that kindly face there was a vague indignation and distress, though it passed almost as our eyes met. Into his there had come a sudden light; he sprang up as one alike rejuvenated and transfigured; there was a quick step in the porch, and next instant the truant Teddy was in our midst.

Mr. Garland met him with outstretched hand but not a question or a syllable of surprise; it was Teddy who uttered the cry of joy, who stood gazing at his father and raining questions upon him as though they had the hall to themselves. What was all this in the evening papers? Who had put it in? Was there any truth in it at all?

"None, Teddy," said Mr. Garland, with some bitterness; "my health was never better in my life."

"Then I can't understand it," cried the son, with savage simplicity. "I suppose it's some rotten practical joke; if so, I would give something to lay hands on the joker!"

His father was still the only one of us he seemed to see, or could bring himself to face in his distress. Not that young Garland had the appearance of one who had been through fresh vicissitudes; on the contrary, he looked both trimmer and ruddier than overnight; and in his sudden fit of passionate indignation, twice the man that one remembered so humiliated and abased.

Raffles came forward from the fireside.

"There are some of us," said he, "who won't be so hard on the beggar for bringing you back from Lord's at last! You must remember that I'm the only one here who has been up there at all, or seen anything of you all day."

Their eyes met; and for one moment I thought that Teddy Garland was going to repudiate this cool *suggestio falsi*, and tell us all where he had really been; but that was now impossible without giving Raffles away, and then there was his Camilla in evident ignorance of the disappearance which he had expected to find common property. The double circumstance was too strong for him; he took her hand with a confused apology which was not even necessary. Anybody could see that the boy had burst among us with eyes for his father only, and thoughts of nothing but the report about his health; as for Miss Belsize, she looked as though she liked him the better for it, or it may have been for an excitability rare in him and rarely becoming. His pink face burnt like a flame. His eyes were brilliant; they met mine at last, and I was warmly greeted; but their friendly light burst into a blaze of wrath as almost simultaneously they fell upon his bugbear in the background.

"So you've kept your threat, Mr. Levy!" said young Garland, quietly enough once he had found his voice.

"I generally do," remarked the money-lender, with a malevolent laugh.

"His threat!" cried Mr. Garland sharply. "What are you talking about, Teddy?"

"I will tell you," said the young man. "And you, too!" he added almost harshly, as Camilla Belsize rose as though about to withdraw. "You may as well know what I am—while there's time. I got into debt—I borrowed from this man."

"You borrowed from him?"

It was Mr. Garland speaking in a voice hard to recognise, with an emphasis harder still to understand; and as he spoke he glared at Levy with new loathing and abhorrence.

"Yes," said Teddy; "he had been pestering me with his beastly circulars every week of my first year at Cambridge. He even wrote to me in his own fist. It was as though he knew something about me and meant getting me in his clutches; and he got me all right in the end, and bled me to the last drop as I deserved. I don't complain so far as I'm concerned. It serves me right. But I did mean to get through without coming to you again, father! I was fool enough to tell him so the other day; that was when he threatened to come to you himself. But I didn't think he was such a brute as to come to-day!"

"Or such a fool?" suggested Raffles, as he put a piece of paper into Teddy's hands.

It was his own original promissory note, the one we had recovered from Dan Levy in the morning. Teddy glanced at it, clutched Raffles by the hand, and went up to the money-lender as though he meant to take him by the throat before us all.

"Does this mean that we're square?" he asked hoarsely.

"It means that you are," replied Dan Levy.

"In fact it amounts to your receipt for every penny I ever owed you?"

"Every penny that you owed me, certainly."

"Yet you must come to my father all the same; you must have it both ways—your money and your spite as well!"

"Put it that way if you like," said Levy, with a shrug of his massive shoulders. "It isn't the case, but what does that matter so long as you're 'appy?"

"No," said Teddy through his teeth; "nothing matters now that I've come back in time."

"In time for what?"

"To turn you out of the house if you don't clear out this instant!"

The great gross man looked upon his athletic young opponent, and folded his arms with a guttural chuckle.

"So you mean to chuck me out, do you?"

"By all my gods, if you make me, Mr. Levy! Here's your hat; there's the door; and never you dare to set foot in this house again."

The money-lender took his shiny topper, gave it a meditative polish with his sleeve, and actually went as bidden to the threshold of the porch; but I saw the suppression of a grin beneath the pendulous nose, a cunning twinkle in the inscrutable eyes, and it did not astonish me when the fellow turned to deliver a Parthian shot. I was only surprised at the harmless character of the shot.

"May I ask whose house it is?" were his words, in themselves notable chiefly for the aspirates of undue deliberation.

"Not mine, I know; but I'm the son of the house," returned Teddy truculently, "and out you go!"

"Are you so sure that it's even your father's house?" inquired Levy with the deadly suavity of which he was capable when he liked. A groan from Mr. Garland confirmed the doubt implied in the words.

"The whole place is his," declared the son, with a sort of nervous scorn—"freehold and everything."

"The whole place happens to be *mine*—'freehold and everything!'" replied Levy, spitting his iced poison in separate syllables. "And as for clearing out, that'll be your job, and I've given you a week to do it in— the two of you!"

He stood a moment in the open doorway, towering in his triumph, glaring on us all in turn, but at Raffles longest and last of all.

"And you needn't think you're going to save the old man," came with a passionate hiss, "like you did the son—*because I know all about you now!*"

VIII

The State of the Case

Of course I made all decent haste from the distressing scene, and of course Raffles stayed behind at the solicitation of his unhappy friends. I was sorry to desert him in view of one aspect of the case; but I was not sorry to dine quietly at the club after the alarms and excitements of that disastrous day. The strain had been the greater after sitting up all night, and I for one could barely realise all that had happened in the twenty-four hours. It seemed incredible that the same midsummer night and day should have seen the return of Raffles and our orgy at the club to which neither of us belonged; the dramatic douche that saluted us at the Albany; the confessions and conferences of the night, the overthrow of the money-lender in the morning; and then the untimely disappearance of Teddy Garland, my day of it at his father's house, and the rain and the ruse that saved the passing situation, only to aggravate the crowning catastrophe of the money-lender's triumph over Raffles and all his friends.

Already a bewildering sequence to look back upon; but it is in the nature of a retrospect to reverse the order of things, and it was the new risk run by Raffles that now loomed largest in my mind, and Levy's last word of warning to him that rang the loudest in my ears. The apparently complete ruin of the Garlands was still a profound mystery to me. But no mere mystery can hold the mind against impending peril; and I was less exercised to account for the downfall of these poor people than in wondering whether it would be followed by that of their friend and mine. Had his Carlsbad crime really found him out? Had Levy only refrained from downright denunciation of Raffles in order to denounce him more effectually to the police? These were the doubts that dogged me at my dinner, and on through the evening until Raffles himself appeared in my corner of the smoking-room, with as brisk a step and as buoyant a countenance as though the whole world and he were one.

"My dear Bunny! I've never given the matter another thought," said he in answer to my nervous queries, "and why the deuce should Dan Levy? He has scored us off quite handsomely as it is; he's not such a fool as to put himself in the wrong by stating what he couldn't possibly prove. They wouldn't listen to him at Scotland Yard; it's not their job, in the first place. And even if it were, no one knows better than our Mr. Shylock that he hasn't a shred of evidence against me."

"Still," said I, "he happens to have hit upon the truth, and that's half the battle in a criminal charge."

"Then it's a battle I should love to fight, if the odds weren't all on Number One! What happens, after all? He recovers his property—he's not a pin the worse off—but because he has a row with me about something else he thinks he can identify me with the Teutonic thief! But not in his heart, Bunny; he's not such a fool as that. Dan Levy's no fool at all, but the most magnificent knave I've been up against yet. If you want to hear all about his tactics, come round to the Albany and I'll open your eyes for you."

His own were radiant with light and life, though he could not have closed them since his arrival at Charing Cross the night before. But midnight was his hour. Raffles was at his best when the stars of the firmament are at theirs; not at Lord's in the light of day, but at dead of night in the historic chambers to which we now repaired. Certainly he had a congenial subject in the celebrated Daniel, "a villain after my own black heart, Bunny! A foeman worthy of Excalibur itself."

And how he longed for the fierce joy of further combat for a bigger stake! But the stake was big enough for even Raffles to shake a hopeless head over it. And his face grew grave as he passed from the fascinating prowess of his enemy to the pitiful position of his friends.

"They said I might tell you, Bunny, but the figures must keep until I have them in black and white. I've promised to see if there really isn't a forlorn hope of getting these poor Garlands out of the spider's web. But there isn't, Bunny, I don't mind telling you."

"What I can't understand," said I, "is how father and son seem to have walked into the same parlour—and the father a business man!"

"Just what he never was," replied Raffles; "that's at the bottom of the whole thing. He was born into a big business, but he wasn't born a business man. So his partners were jolly glad to buy him out some years ago; and then it was that poor old Garland lashed out into the place where you spent the day, Bunny. It has been his ruin. The price was pretty stiff to start with; you might have a house in most squares and quite a good place in the country for what you've got to pay for a cross between the two. But the mixture was exactly what attracted these good people; for it was not only in Mrs. Garland's time, but it seems she was the first to set her heart upon the place. So she was the first to leave it for a better world—poor soul—before the glass was on the last vinery. And the poor old boy was left to pay the shot alone."

"I wonder he didn't get rid of the whole show," said I, "after that."

"I've no doubt he felt like it, Bunny, but you don't get rid of a place like that in five minutes; it's neither fish nor flesh; the ordinary house-hunter, with the money to spend, wants to be nearer in or further out. On the other hand there was a good reason for holding on. That part of Kensington is being gradually rebuilt; old Garland had bought the freehold, and sooner or later it was safe to sell at a handsome profit for building sites. That was the one excuse for his dip; it was really a fine investment, or would have been if he had left more margin for upkeep and living expenses. As it was he soon found himself a bit of a beggar on horseback. And instead of selling his horse at a sacrifice, he put him at a fence that's brought down many a better rider."

"What was that?"

"South Africans!" replied Raffles succinctly. "Piles were changing hands over them at the time, and poor old Garland began with a lucky dip himself; that finished him off. There's no tiger like an old tiger that never tasted blood before. Our respected brewer became a reckless gambler, lashed at everything, and in due course omitted to cover his losses. They were big enough to ruin him, without being enormous. Thousands were wanted at almost a moment's notice; no time to fix up an honest mortgage; it was a case of pay, fail, or borrow through the nose! And old Garland took ten thousand of the best from Dan Levy—and had another dip!"

"And lost again?"

"And lost again, and borrowed again, this time on the security of his house; and the long and short of it is that he and every stick, brick and branch he is supposed to possess have been in Dan Levy's hands for months and years."

"On a sort of mortgage?"

"On a perfectly nice and normal mortgage so far as interest went, only with a power to call in the money after six months. But old Garland is being bled to the heart for iniquitous interest on the first ten thousand, and of course he can't meet the call for another fifteen when it comes; but he thinks it's all right because Levy doesn't press for the dibs. Of course it's all wrong from that moment. Levy has the right to take possession whenever he jolly well likes; but it doesn't suit him to have the place empty on his hands, it might depreciate a rising property, and so poor old Garland is deliberately lulled into a false sense of security. And there's no saying how long that state of things might have lasted if we hadn't taken a rise out of old Shylock this morning."

"Then it's our fault, A.J.?"

"It's mine," said Raffles remorsefully. "The idea, I believe, was altogether mine, Bunny; that's why I'd give my bowing hand to take the old ruffian at his word, and save the governor as we did the boy!"

"But how *do* you account for his getting them both into his toils?" I asked. "What was the point of lending heavily to the son when the father already owed more than he could pay?"

"There are so many points," said Raffles. "They love you to owe more than you can pay; it's not their principal that they care about nearly so much as your interest; what they hate is to lose you when once they've got you. In this case Levy would see how frightfully keen poor old Garland was about his boy—to do him properly and, above all, not to let him see what an effort it's become. Levy would find out something about the boy; that he's getting hard up himself, that he's bound to discover the old man's secret, and capable of making trouble and spoiling things when he does. 'Better give him the same sort of secret of his own to keep,' says Levy, 'then they'll both hold their tongues, and I'll have one of 'em under each thumb till all's blue.' So he goes for Teddy till he gets him, and finances father and son in watertight compartments until this libel case comes along and does make things look a bit blue for once. Not blue enough, mind you, to compel the sale of a big rising property at a sacrifice; but the sort of thing to make a man squeeze his small creditors all round, while still nursing his top class. So you see how it all fits in. They say the old blackguard is briefing Mr. Attorney himself; that along with all the rest to scale, will run him into thousands even if he wins his case."

"May he lose it!" said I, drinking devoutly, while Raffles lit the inevitable Egyptian. I gathered that this plausible exposition of Mr. Levy's tactics had some foundation in the disclosures of his hapless friends; but his ready grasp of an alien subject was highly characteristic of Raffles. I said I supposed Miss Belsize had not remained to hear the whole humiliating story, but Raffles replied briefly that she had. By putting the words into his mouth, I now learnt that she had taken the whole trouble as finely as I should somehow have expected from those fearless eyes of hers; that Teddy had offered to release her on the spot, and that Camilla Belsize had refused to be released; but when I applauded her spirit, Raffles was ostentatiously irresponsive. Nothing, indeed, could have been more marked than the contrast between his reluctance to discuss Miss Belsize and the captious gusto with which she had discussed him. But in each case the inference was that there was no love lost between the pair; and in each case I could not help wondering why.

There was, however, another subject upon which Raffles exercised a much more vexatious reserve. Had I been more sympathetically interested in Teddy Garland, no doubt I should have sought an earlier explanation of his sensational disappearance, instead of leaving it to the last. My interest in the escapade, however, was considerably quickened by the prompt refusal of Raffles to tell me a word about it.

"No, Bunny," said he, "I'm not going to give the boy away. His father knows, and I know—and that's enough."

"Was it your paragraph in the papers that brought him back?"

Raffles paused, cigarette between fingers, in a leonine perambulation of his cage; and his smile was a sufficient affirmative.

"I mustn't talk about it, really, Bunny," was his actual reply. "It wouldn't be fair."

"I don't think it's conspicuously fair on me," I retorted, "to set me to cover up your pal's tracks, to give me a lie like that to act all day, and then not to take one into the secret when he does turn up. I call it trading on a fellow's good-nature—not that I care a curse!"

"Then that's all right, Bunny," said Raffles genially. "If you cared I should feel bound to apologise to you for the very rotten way you've been treated all round; as it is I give you my word not to take you in with me if I have another dip at Dan Levy."

"But you're not seriously thinking of it, Raffles?"

"I am if I see half a chance of squaring him short of wilful murder."

"You mean a chance of settling his account against the Garlands?"

"To say nothing of my own account against Dan Levy! I'm spoiling for another round with that sportsman, Bunny, for its own sake quite apart from these poor pals of mine."

"And you really think the game would be worth a candle that might fire the secret mine of your life and blow your character to blazes?"

One could not fraternise with Raffles without contracting a certain facility in fluent and florid metaphor; and this parody of his lighter manner drew a smile from my model. But it was the bleak smile of a man thinking of other things, and I thought he nodded rather sadly. He was standing by the open window; he turned and leant out as I had done that interminable twenty-four hours ago; and I longed to know his thoughts, to guess what it was that I knew he had not told me, that I could not divine for myself. There was something behind his mask of gay pugnacity; nay, there was something behind the good Garlands and their culpably commonplace misfortunes. They were the pretext. But could they be the Cause?

The night was as still as the night before. In another moment a flash might have enlightened me. But, in the complete cessation of sound in the room, I suddenly heard one, soft and stealthy but quite distinct, outside the door.

IX

A Triple Alliance

It was the intermittent sound of cautious movements, the creak of a sole not repeated for a great many seconds, the all but inaudible passing of a hand over the unseen side of the door leading into the lobby. It may be that I imagined more than I actually heard of the last detail; nevertheless I was as sure of what was happening as though the door had been plate-glass. Yet there was the outer door between lobby and landing and that I distinctly remembered Raffles shutting behind him when we entered. Unable to attract his attention now, and never sorry to be the one to take the other by surprise, I listened without breathing until assurance was doubly sure, then bounded out of my chair without a word. And there was a resounding knock at the inner door, even as I flung it open upon a special evening edition of Mr. Daniel Levy, a resplendent figure with a great stud blazing in a frilled shirt, white waistcoat and gloves, opera-hat and cigar, and all the other insignia of a nocturnal vulgarian about town.

"May I come in?" said he with unctuous affability.

"May you!" I took it upon myself to shout. "I like that, seeing that you came in long ago! I heard you all right—you were listening at the door—probably looking through the keyhole—and you only knocked when I jumped up to open it!"

"My dear Bunny!" exclaimed Raffles, a reproving hand upon my shoulder. And he bade the unbidden guest a jovial welcome.

"But the outer door was shut," I expostulated. "He must have forced it or else picked the lock."

"Why not, Bunny? Love isn't the only thing that laughs at locksmiths," remarked Raffles with exasperating geniality.

"Neither are swell mobsmen!" cried Dan Levy, not more ironically than Raffles, only with a heavier type of irony.

Raffles conducted him to a chair. Levy stepped behind it and grasped the back as though prepared to break the furniture on our heads if necessary. Raffles offered him a drink; it was declined with a crafty grin that made no secret of a base suspicion.

"I don't drink with the swell mob," said the money-lender.

"My dear Mr. Levy," returned Raffles, "you're the very man I wanted to see, and nobody could possibly be more welcome in my humble quarters; but that's the fourth time to-day I've heard you make use of an obsolete expression. You know as well as I do that the slap-bang-here-we-are-again type of work is a thing of the past. Where are the jolly dogs of the old song now?"

"'Ere at the Albany!" said Levy. "Here in your rooms, Mr. A.J. Raffles."

"Well, Bunny," said Raffles, "I suppose we must both plead guilty to a hair of the jolly dog that bit him—eh?"

"You know what I mean," our visitor ground out through his teeth. "You're cracksmen, magsmen, mobsmen, the two of you; so you may as well both own up to it."

"Cracksmen? Magsmen? Mobsmen?" repeated Raffles, with his head on one side. "What does the kind gentleman mean, Bunny? Wait! I have it—thieves! Common thieves!"

And he laughed loud and long in the moneylender's face and mine.

"You may laugh," said Levy. "I'm too old a bird for your chaff; the only wonder is I didn't spot you right off when we were abroad." He grinned malevolently. "Shall I tell you when I did tumble to it—Mr. Ananias J. Raffles?"

"Daniel in the liars' den," murmured Raffles, wiping the tears from his eyes. "Oh, yes, do tell us anything you like; this is the best entertainment we've had for a long time, isn't it, Bunny?"

"Chalks!" said I.

"I thought of it this morning," proceeded the money-lender, with a grim contempt for all our raillery, "when you played your pretty trick upon me, so glib and smooth, and up to every move, the pair of you! One borrowing the money, and the other paying me back in my very own actual coin!"

"Well," said I, "there was no crime in that."

"Oh, yes, there was," replied Levy, with a wide wise grin; "there was the one crime you two ought to know better than ever to commit, if you call yourselves what I called you just now. The crime that you committed was the crime of being found out; but for that I should never have suspected friend Ananias of that other job at Carlsbad; no, not even when I saw his friends so surprised to hear that he'd been out there—a strapping young chap like 'im! Yes," cried the money-lender, lifting the chair and jobbing it down on the floor;

"this morning was when I thought of it, but this afternoon was when I jolly well knew."

Raffles was no longer smiling; his eyes were like points of steel, his lips like a steel trap.

"I saw what you thought," said he, disdainfully. "And you still seriously think I took your wife's necklace and hid it in the woods?"

"I know you did."

"Then what the devil are you doing here alone?" cried Raffles. "Why didn't you bring along a couple of good men and true from Scotland Yard? Here I am, Mr. Levy, entirely at your service. Why don't you give me in charge?"

Levy chuckled consumedly—ventriloquously—behind his three gold buttons and his one diamond stud.

"P'r'aps I'm not such a bad sort as you think," said he. "An' p'r'aps you two gentlemen are not such bad sorts as *I* thought."

"Gentlemen once more, eh?" said Raffles. "Isn't that rather a quick recovery for swell magsmen, or whatever we were a minute ago?"

"P'r'aps I never really thought you quite so bad as all that, Mr. Raffles."

"Perhaps you never really thought I took the necklace, Mr. Levy?"

"I know you took it," returned Levy, his new tone of crafty conciliation softening to a semblance of downright apology. "But I believe you did put it back where you knew it'd be found. And I begin to think you only took it for a bit o' fun!"

"If he took it at all," said I. "Which is absurd."

"I only wish I had!" exclaimed Raffles, with gratuitous audacity. "I agree with you, Mr. Levy, it would have been more like a bit of fun than anything that came my way on the human rubbish-heap we were both inhabiting for our sins."

"The kind of fun that appeals to you?" suggested Levy, with a very shrewd glance.

"It would," said Raffles, "I feel sure."

"'Ow would you care for another bit o' fun like it, Mr. Raffles?"

"Don't say 'another,' please."

"Well, would you like to try your 'and at the game again?"

"Not 'again,' Mr. Levy; and my 'prentice' hand, if you don't mind."

"I beg pardon; my mistake," said Levy, with becoming gravity.

"How would I like to try my prentice hand on picking and stealing for the pure fun of the thing? Is that it, Mr. Levy?"

Raffles was magnificent now; but so was the other in his own way. And once more I could but admire the tact with which Levy had discarded his favourite cudgels, and the surprising play that he was making with the buttoned foil.

"It'd be more picking than stealing," said he. "Tricky picking too, Raffles, but innocent enough even for an amatoor."

"I thank you, Mr. Levy. So you have a definite case in mind?"

"I have—a case of recovering a man's own property."

"You being the man, Mr. Levy?"

"I being the man, Mr. Raffles."

"Bunny, I begin to see why he didn't bring the police with him!"

I affected to have seen it for some time; thereupon our friend the enemy protested that in no circumstances could he have taken such a course. By the searchlight of the present he might have detected things which had entirely escaped his notice in the past—incriminating things—things that would put together into a Case. But, after all, what evidence had he against Raffles as yet? Mr. Levy himself propounded the question with unflinching candour. He might inform the Metropolitan Police of his strong suspicions; and they might communicate with the Austrian police, and evidence beyond the belated evidence of his own senses be duly forthcoming; but nothing could be done at once, and if Raffles cared to endorse his theory of the practical joke, by owning up to that and nothing more, then, so far as Mr. Levy was concerned, nothing should ever be done at all.

"Except this little innocent recovery of your own property," suggested Raffles. "I suppose that's the condition?"

"Condition's not the word I should have employed," said Levy, with a shrug.

"Preliminary, then?"

"Indemnity is more the idea. You put me to a lot of trouble by abstracting Mrs. Levy's jewels for your own amusement—"

"So you assert, Mr. Levy."

"Well, I may be wrong; that remains to be seen—or not—as you decide," rejoined the Jew, lifting his mask for the moment. "At all events you admit that it's the sort of adventure you would like to try. And so I ask you to amuse yourself by abstracting something else of mine that 'appens to have got into the wrong hands; then, I say, we shall be quits."

"Well," said Raffles, "there's no harm in our hearing what sort of property it is, and where you think it's to be found."

The usurer leant forward in his chair; he had long been sitting in the one which at first he had seemed inclined to wield as a defensive weapon. We all drew together into a smaller triangle. And I found our visitor looking specially hard at me for the first time.

"I've seen you, too, before to-day," said he. "I thought I had, after you'd gone this morning, and when we met in the afternoon I made sure. It was at the Savoy when me and my wife were dining there and you gentlemen were at the next table." There was a crafty twinkle in his eye, but the natural allusion to the necklace was not made. "I suppose," he continued, "you are partners in—amusement? Otherwise I should insist on speaking to Mr. Raffles alone."

"Bunny and I are one," said Raffles airily.

"Though two to one—numerically speaking," remarked Levy, with a disparaging eye on me. "However, if you're both in the job, so much the more chance of bringing it off, I daresay. But you'll never 'ave to 'andle a lighter swag, gentlemen!"

"More jewellery?" inquired Raffles, as one thoroughly enjoying the joke.

"No—lighter than that—a letter!"

"One little letter?"

"That's all."

"Of your own writing, Mr. Levy?"

"No, sir!" thundered the money-lender, just when I could have sworn his lips were framing an affirmative.

"I see; it was written to you, not by you."

"Wrong again, Raffles!"

"Then how can the letter be your property, my dear Mr. Levy?"

There was a pause. The money-lender was at visible grips with some new difficulty. I watched his heavy but not unhandsome face, and timed the moment of mastery by the sudden light in his crafty eyes.

"They think it was written by me," said he. "It's a forgery, written on my office paper; if that isn't my property, I should like to know what is?"

"It certainly ought to be," returned Raffles, sympathetically. "Of course you're speaking of the crucial letter in your case against *Fact*?"

"I am," said Levy, rather startled; "but 'ow did you know I was?"

"I am naturally interested in the case."

"And you've read about it in the papers; they've had a fat sight too much to say about it, with the whole case still *sub judice*."

"I read the original articles in *Fact*," said Raffles.

"And the letters I'm supposed to have written?"

"Yes; there was only one of them that struck me as being slap in the wind's eye."

"That's the one I want."

"If it's genuine, Mr. Levy, it might easily form the basis of a more serious sort of case."

"But it isn't genuine."

"Nor would you be the first plaintiff in the High Court of Justice," pursued Raffles, blowing soft grey rings into the upper air, "who has been rather rudely transformed into the defendant at the Old Bailey."

"But it isn't genuine, I'm telling you!" cried Dan Levy with a curse.

"Then what in the world do you want with the letter? Let the prosecution love and cherish it, and trump it up in court for all it's worth; the less it is worth, the more certain to explode and blow their case to bits. A palpable forgery in the hands of Mr. Attorney!" cried Raffles, with a wink at me. "It'll be the best fun of its kind since the late lamented Mr. Pigott; my dear Bunny, we must both be there."

Mr. Levy's uneasiness was a sight for timid eyes. He had presented his case to us naked and unashamed; already he was in our hands more surely than Raffles was in his. But Raffles was the last person to betray his sense of an advantage a second too soon: he merely gave me another wink. The usurer was frowning at the carpet. Suddenly he sprang up and burst out in a bitter tirade upon the popular and even the judicial prejudice against his own beneficent calling. No money-lender would ever get justice in a British court of law; easier for the camel to thread the needle's eye. That flagrant forgery would be accepted at sight by our vaunted British jury. The only chance was to abstract it before the case came on.

"But if it can be proved to be a forgery," urged Raffles, "nothing could possibly turn the tables on the other side with such complete and instantaneous effect."

"I've told you what I reckon my only chance," said Levy fiercely. "Let me remind you that it's yours as well!"

"If you talk like that," said Raffles, "I shan't consider it."

"You won't in any case, I should hope," said I.

"Oh, yes, I might; but not if he talks like that."

Levy stopped talking quite like that.

"Will you do it, Mr. Raffles, or will you not?"

"Abstract the—forgery?"

"Yes."

"Where from?"

"Wherever it may be; their solicitors' safe, I suppose."

"Who are the solicitors to *Fact*?"

"Burroughs and Burroughs."

"Of Gray's Inn Square?"

"That's right."

"The strongest firm in England for a criminal case," said Raffles, with a grimace at me. "Their strong-room is probably the strongest strong-room!"

"I said it was a tricky job," rejoined the moneylender.

Raffles looked more than dubious.

"Big game for a first shoot, eh, Bunny?"

"Too big by half."

"And you merely wish to have their letter—withdrawn, Mr. Levy?"

"That's the way to put it."

And the diamond stud sparkled again as it heaved upon the billows of an intestine chuckle.

"Withdrawn—and nothing more?"

"That'll be good enough for me, Mr. Raffles."

"Even though they miss it the very next morning?"

"Let them miss it."

Raffles joined his finger-tips judicially, and shook his head in serene dissent.

"It would do you more harm than good, Mr. Levy. I should be inclined to go one better—if I went into the thing at all," he added, with so much point that I was thankful to think he was beginning to decide against it.

"What improvement do you suggest?" inquired Dan Levy, who had evidently no such premonition.

"I should take a sheet of your paper with me, and forge the forgery!" said Raffles, a light in his eye and a gusto in his voice that I knew only too well. "But I shouldn't do my work as perfectly as—the other cove—did his. My effort would look the same as yours—*his*—until Mr. Attorney fixed it with his eyeglass in open court. And then the bottom would be out of the defence in five minutes!"

Dan Levy came straight over to Raffles—quivering like a jelly—beaming at every pore.

"Shake!" he cried. "I always knew you were a man after my own heart, but I didn't know you were a man of genius until this minute."

"It's no use my shaking," replied Raffles, the tips of his sensitive fingers still together, "until I make up my mind to take on the job. And I'm a very long way from doing that yet, Mr. Levy."

I breathed again.

"But you must, my dear friend, you simply must!" said Levy, in a new tone of pure persuasion. I was sorry he forgot to threaten instead. Perhaps it was not forgetfulness; perhaps he was beginning to know his Raffles as I knew mine; if so, I was sorrier still.

"It's a case of *quid pro quo*," said Raffles calmly. "You can't expect me to break out into downright crime—however technical the actual offence—unless you make it worth my while."

Levy became the man I wanted him to be again. "I fancy it's worth your while not to hear anything more about Carlsbad," said he, though still with less of the old manner than I could have wished.

"What!" cried Raffles, "when you own yourself that you've no evidence against me there?"

"Evidence is to be got that may mean five years to you; don't you make any mistake about that."

"Whereas the evidence of this particular letter against yourself has, on your own showing, already been obtained! It's as you like, of course," added Raffles, getting up with a shrug. "But if the Old Bailey sees us both, Mr. Levy, I'll back my chance against yours—and your sentence against mine!"

Raffles helped himself to a drink, after a quizzical look at his guest, decanter in hand; the usurer snatched it from him and splashed out half a tumbler. Certainly he was beginning to know his Raffles perilously well.

"There, damn you!" said he, blinking into an empty glass. "I trust you further than I'd trust any other young blood of your kidney; name your price, and you shall earn it if you can."

"You may think it a rather long one, Mr. Levy."

"Never mind; you say what you want."

"Leave that money of yours on the mortgage with Mr. Garland; forgive him his other debt as you hope to be forgiven; and either that letter shall be in your hands, or I'll be in the hands of the police, before a week is up!"

Spoken from man to man with equal austerity and resolution, yet in a voice persuasive and conciliatory rather than arbitrary or dictatorial, the mere form and manner of this quixotic undertaking thrilled all my fibres in defiance of its sense. It was like the blare of bugles in a dubious cause; one's blood responded before one's brain; and but for Raffles, little as his friends were to me, and much as I repudiated his sacrifices on their behalf, that very minute I might have led the first assault on their oppressor. In a sudden fury the savage had hurled his empty tumbler into the fireplace, and followed the crash with such a volley of abuse as I have seldom heard from human brute.

"I'm surprised at you, Mr. Levy," said Raffles, contemptuously; "if we copied your tactics we should throw you through that open window!"

And I stood by for my share in the deed.

"Yes! I know it'd pay you to break my neck," retorted Levy. "You'd rather swing than do time, wouldn't you?"

"And you prefer the other alternative," said Raffles, "to loosing your grip upon a man who's done you no harm whatever! In interest alone he's almost repaid all you lent him in the first instance; you've first-class security for the rest; yet you must ruin him to revenge yourself upon us. On us, mark you! It's against us you've got your grievance, not against old Garland or his son. You've lost sight of that fact. That little trick this morning was our doing entirely. Why don't you take it out of us? Why refuse a fair offer to spite people who have done you no harm?"

"It's not a fair offer," growled Levy. "I made you the fair offer."

But his rage had moderated; he was beginning to listen to Raffles and to reason, with however ill a grace. It was the very moment which Raffles was the very man to improve.

"Mr. Levy," said he, "do you suppose I care whether you hold your tongue or not on a matter of mere suspicion, which you can't support by a grain of evidence? You lose a piece of jewellery abroad; you recover it intact; and after many days you get the bright idea that I'm the culprit because I happen to have been staying in your hotel at the time. It never occurred to you there or then, though you interviewed the gentleman face to face, as you were constantly interviewing me. But as soon as I borrow some money from you, here in London in the ordinary way, you say I must be the man who borrowed Mrs. Levy's necklace in that extraordinary way at Carlsbad! I should say it to the marines, Mr. Levy, if I were you; they're the only force that are likely to listen to you."

"I do say it, all the same; and what's more you don't deny it. If you weren't the man you wouldn't be so ready for another game like it now."

"Ready for it?" cried Raffles, more than ready for an undeniable point. "I'm always your man for a new sensation, Mr. Levy, and for years I've taken an academic interest in the very fine art of burglary; isn't that so, Bunny?"

"I've often heard you say so," I replied without mishap.

"In these piping times," continued Raffles, "it's about the one exciting and romantic career open to us. If it were not so infernally dishonest I should have half a mind to follow it myself. And here you come and put up a crib for me to crack in the best interests of equity and justice; not to enrich the wicked cracksman, but to restore his rightful property to the honest financier; a sort of teetotal felony—the very ginger-ale of crime! Is that a beverage to refuse—a chance to miss—a temptation to resist? Yet the risks are just as great as if it were a fine old fruity felony; you can't expect me to run them for nothing, or even for their own exciting sake. You know my terms, Mr. Levy; if you don't accept them, it's already two in the morning, and I should like to get to bed before it's light."

"And if I did accept them?" said Levy, after a considerable pause.

"The letter to which you attach such importance would most probably be in your possession by the beginning of next week."

"And I should have to take my hands off a nice little property that has tumbled into them?"

"Only for a time," said Raffles. "On the other hand, you would be permanently out of danger of figuring in the dock on a charge of blackmail. And you know your profession isn't popular in the courts, Mr. Levy; it's in nearly as bad odour as the crime of blackmail!"

A singular docility had descended like a mantle upon Daniel Levy: no uncommon reaction in the case of very passionate men, and yet in this case ominous, sinister, and completely unconvincing so far as I personally was concerned. I longed to tell Raffles what I thought, to put him on his guard against his obvious superior in low cunning. But Raffles would not even catch my eye. And already he looked insanely pleased with himself and his apparent advantage.

"Will you give me until to-morrow morning?" said Levy, taking up his hat.

"If you mean the morning; by eleven I must be at Lord's."

"Say ten o'clock in Jermyn Street?"

"It's a strange bargain, Mr. Levy. I should prefer to clinch it out of earshot of your clerks."

"Then I will come here."

"I shall be ready for you at ten."

"And alone?"

There was a sidelong glance at me with the proviso.

"You shall search the premises yourself and seal up all the doors."

"Meanwhile," said Levy, putting on his hat, "I shall think about it, but that's all. I haven't agreed yet, Mr. Raffles; don't you make too sure that I ever shall. I shall think about it—but don't you make too sure."

He was gone like a lamb, this wild beast of five minutes back. Raffles showed him out, and down into the courtyard, and out again into Piccadilly. There was no question but that he was gone for good; back came Raffles, rubbing his hands for joy.

"A fine night, Bunny! A finer day to follow! But a nice, slow, wicket-keeper's wicket if ever Teddy had one in his life!"

I came to my point with all vehemence.

"Confound Teddy!" I cried from my heart. "I should have thought you had run risks enough for his sake as it was!"

"How do you know it's for his sake—or anybody's?" asked Raffles, quite hotly. "Do you suppose I want to be beaten by a brute like Levy, Garlands or no Garlands? Besides, there's far less risk in what I mean to do than in what I've been doing; at all events it's in my line."

"It's not in your line," I retorted, "to strike a bargain with a swine who won't dream of keeping his side."

"I shall make him," said Raffles. "If he won't do what I want he shan't have what he wants."

"But how could you trust him to keep his word?"

"His word!" cried Raffles, in ironical echo. "We shall have to carry matters far beyond his word, of course; deeds, not words, Bunny, and the deeds properly prepared by solicitors and executed by Dan Levy before he lays a finger on his own blackmailing letter. You remember old Mother Hubbard in our house at school? He's a little solicitor somewhere in the City; he'll throw the whole thing into legal shape for us, and ask no questions and tell no tales. You leave Mr. Shylock to me and Mother, and we'll bring him up to the scratch as he ought to go."

There was no arguing with Raffles in such a mood; argue I did, but he paid no attention to what I said. He had unlocked a drawer in the bureau, and taken out a map that I had never seen before. I looked over his shoulder as he spread it out in the light of his reading-lamp. And it was a map of London capriciously sprinkled with wheels and asterisks of red ink; there was a finished wheel in Bond Street, another in Half-Moon Street, one on the site of Thornaby House, Park Lane, and others as remote as St. John's Wood and Peter Street, Campden Hill; the asterisks were fewer, and I have less reason to remember their latitude and longitude.

"What's this, A.J.?" I asked. "It looks exactly like a war-map."

"It is one, Bunny," said he; "it's the map of one man's war against the ordered forces of society. The spokes are only the scenes of future operations, but each finished wheel marks the field of some past engagement, in which you have usually been the one man's one and only accomplice."

And he stooped and drew the neatest of blood-red asterisks at the southern extremity of Gray's Inn Square.

X

"My Raffles Right or Wrong"

The historic sward had just been cleared for action when Raffles and I met at Lord's next day. I blush to own I had been knave and fool enough to suggest that he should smuggle me into the pavilion; but perhaps the only laws of man that Raffles really respected were those of the M.C.C., and it was in Block B. that he joined me a minute or so before eleven. The sun was as strong and the sky as blue as though the disastrous day before had been just such another. But its tropical shower-bath had left the London air as cleanly and as clear as crystal; the neutral tints of every day were splashes of vivid colour, the waiting umpires animated snow-men, the heap of sawdust at either end a pyramid of powdered gold upon an emerald ground. And in the expectant hush before the appearance of the fielding side, I still recall the Yorkshire accent of the Surrey Poet, hawking his latest lyric on some "Great Stand by Mr. Webbe and Mr. Stoddart," and incidentally assuring the crowd that Cambridge was going to win because everybody said Oxford would.

"Just in time," said Raffles, as he sat down and the Cambridge men emerged from the pavilion, capped and sashed in varying shades of light blue. The captain's colours were bleached by service; but the wicket-keeper's were the newest and the bluest of the lot, and as a male historian I shrink from saying how well they suited him.

"Teddy Garland looks as though nothing had happened," was what I said at the time, as I peered through my binocular at the padded figure with the pink face and the gigantic gloves.

"That's because he knows there's a chance of nothing more happening," was the reply. "I've seen him and his poor old governor up here since I saw Dan Levy."

I eagerly inquired as to the upshot of the earlier interview, but Raffles looked as though he had not heard. The Oxford captain had come out to open the innings with a player less known to fame; the first ball of the match hurtled down the pitch, and the Oxford captain left it severely alone. Teddy took it charmingly, and almost with the same movement the ball was back in the bowler's hands.

"*He's* all right!" muttered Raffles with a long breath. "So is our Mr. Shylock, Bunny; we fixed things up in no time after all. But the worst of it is I shall only be able to stop—"

He broke off, mouth open as it might have been mine. A ball had been driven hard to extra cover, and quite well fielded; another had been taken by Teddy as competently as the first, but not returned to the bowler. The Oxford captain had played at it, and we heard something even in Block B.

"How's that?" came almost simultaneously in Teddy's ringing voice. Up went the umpire's finger, and down came Raffles's hand upon my thigh.

"He's caught him, Bunny!" he cried in my ear above the Cambridge cheers. "The best bat on either side, and Teddy's outed him third ball!" He stopped to watch the defeated captain's slow return, the demonstration on the pitch in Teddy's honour; then he touched me on the arm and dropped his voice. "He's forgotten all his troubles now, Bunny, if you like; nothing's going to worry him till lunch, unless he misses a sitting chance. And he won't, you'll see; a good start means even more behind the sticks than in front of 'em."

Raffles was quite right. Another wicket fell cheaply in another way; then came a long spell of plucky cricket, a stand not masterly but dogged and judicious, in which many a ball outside the off-stump was allowed to pass unmolested, and a few were unfortunate in just beating the edge of the bat. On the tricky wicket Teddy's work was cut out for him, and beautifully he did it. It was a treat to see his lithe form crouching behind the bails, to rise next instant with the rising ball; his great gloves were always in the right place, always adhesive. Once only he held them up prematurely, and a fine ball brushed the wicket on its way for four byes; it was his sole error all the morning. Raffles sat enchanted; so in truth did I; but between the overs I endeavoured to obtain particulars of his latest parley with Dan Levy, and once or twice extracted a stray detail.

"The old sinner has a place on the river, Bunny, though I have my suspicions of a second establishment nearer town. But I'm to find him at his lawful home all the next few nights, and sitting up for me till two in the morning."

"Then you're going to Gray's Inn Square this week?"

"I'm going there this morning for a peep at the crib; there's no time to be lost, but on the other hand there's a devil of a lot to learn. I say, Bunny, there's going to be another change of bowling; the fast stuff, too, by Jove!"

E.W. HORNUNG

A massive youth had taken the ball at the top end, and the wicket-keeper was retiring to a more respectful distance behind the stumps.

"You'll let me know when it's to be?" I whispered, but Raffles only answered, "I wonder Jack Studley didn't wait till there was more of a crust on the mud pie. That tripe's no use without a fast wicket!"

The technical slang of the modern cricket-field is ever a weariness; at the moment it was something worse, and I resigned myself to the silent contemplation of as wild an over as ever was bowled at Lord's. A shocking thing to the off was sent skipping past point for four. "Tripe!" muttered Raffles to himself. A very good one went over the bails and thud into Garland's gloves like a round-shot. "Well bowled!" said Raffles with less reserve. Another delivery was merely ignored, both at the wicket and at my side, and then came a high full-pitch to leg which the batsman hit hard but very late. It was a hit that might have smashed the pavilion palings. But it never reached them; it stuck in Teddy's left glove instead, and none of us knew it till we saw him staggering towards long-leg, and tossing up the ball as he recovered balance.

"That's the worst ball that ever took a wicket in this match!" vowed a reverend veteran as the din died down.

"And the best catch!" cried Raffles. "Come on, Bunny; that's my *nunc dimittis* for the day. There would be nothing to compare with it if I could stop to see every ball bowled, and I mustn't see another."

"But why?" I asked, as I followed Raffles into the press behind the carriages.

"I've already told you why," said he.

I got as close to him as one could in that crowd.

"You're not thinking of doing it to-night, A.J.?"

"I don't know."

"But you'll let *me* know?"

"Not if I can help it, Bunny; didn't I promise not to drag you any further through this particular mire?"

"But if *I* can help *you*?" I whispered, after a momentary separation in the throng.

"Oh! if I can't get on without you," said Raffles, not nicely, "I'll let you know fast enough. But do drop the subject now; here come old Garland and Camilla Belsize!"

They did not see us quite so soon as we saw them, and for a moment one felt a spy; but it was an interesting moment even to a person smarting from a snub. The ruined man looked haggard, ill, unfit to be about, the very embodiment of the newspaper report concerning him. But the spirit beamed through the shrinking flesh, the poor old fellow was alight with pride and love, exultant in spite of himself and his misfortunes. He had seen his boy's great catch; he had heard the cheers, he would hear them till his dying hour. Camilla Belsize had also seen and heard, but not with the same exquisite appreciation. Cricket was a game to her, it was not that quintessence and epitome of life it would seem to be to some of its devotees; and real life was pressing so heavily upon her that the trivial consolation which had banished her companion's load could not lighten hers. So at least I thought as they approached, the man so worn and radiant, the girl so pensive for all her glorious youth and beauty: his was the old head bowed with sorrow, his also the simpler and the younger heart.

"That catch will console me for a lot," I heard him say quite heartily to Raffles. But Camilla's comment was altogether perfunctory; indeed, I wondered that so sophisticated a person did not affect some little enthusiasm. She seemed more interested, however, in the crowd than in the cricket. And that was usual enough.

Raffles was already saying he must go, with an explanatory murmur to Mr. Garland, who clasped his hand with a suddenly clouded countenance. But Miss Belsize only bowed, and scarcely took her eyes off a couple of outwardly inferior men, who had attracted my attention through hers, until they also passed out of the ground.

Mr. Garland was on tip-toes watching the game again with mercurial ardour.

"Mr. Manders will look after me," she said to him, "won't you, Mr. Manders?" I made some suitable asseveration, and she added: "Mr. Garland's a member, you know, and dying to go into the Pavilion."

"Only just to hear what they think of Teddy," the poor old boy confessed; and when we had arranged where to meet in the interval, away he hurried with his keen, worn face.

Miss Belsize turned to me the moment he was gone.

"I want to speak to you, Mr. Manders," she said quickly but without embarrassment. "Where can we talk?"

"And watch as well?" I suggested, thinking of the young man at his best behind the sticks.

"I want to speak to you first," she said, "where we shan't be overheard. It's about Mr. Raffles!" added Miss Belsize as she met my stare.

About Raffles again! About Raffles, after all that she had learnt the day before! I did not enjoy the prospect as I led the way past the ivy-mantled tennis-court of those days to the practice-ground, turned for the nonce into a tented lawn.

"And what about Raffles?" I asked as we struck out for ourselves across the grass.

"I'm afraid he's in some danger," replied Miss Belsize. And she stopped in her walk and confronted me as frankly as though we had the animated scene to ourselves.

"Danger!" I repeated, guiltily enough, no doubt. "What makes you think that, Miss Belsize?"

My companion hesitated for the first time.

"You won't tell him I told you, Mr. Manders?"

"Not if you don't want me to," said I, taken aback more by her manner than by the request itself.

"You promise me that?"

"Certainly."

"Then tell me, did you notice two men who passed close to us just after we had all met?"

"There are so many men to notice," said I to gain time.

"But these were not the sort one expects to see here to-day."

"Did they wear bowlers and short coats?"

"You did notice them!"

"Only because I saw you watching them," said I, recalling the whole scene.

"They wanted watching," rejoined Miss Belsize dryly. "They followed Mr. Raffles out of the ground!"

"So they did!" I reflected aloud in my alarm.

"They were following you both when you met us."

"The dickens they were! Was that the first you saw of them?"

"No; the first time was over there at the nets before play began. I noticed those two men behind Teddy's net. They were not watching him; that called my attention to them. It's my belief they were lying in wait for Mr. Raffles; at any rate, when he came they moved away. But they followed us afterwards across the ground."

"You are sure of that?"

"I looked round to see," said Miss Belsize, avoiding my eyes for the first time.

"Did you think the men—detectives?"

And I forced a laugh.

"I was afraid they might be, Mr. Manders, though I have never seen one off the stage."

"Still," I pursued, with painfully sustained amusement, "you were ready to find A.J. Raffles being shadowed here at Lord's of all places in the world?"

"I was ready for anything, anywhere," said Miss Belsize, "after all I heard yesterday afternoon."

"You mean about poor Mr. Garland and his affairs?"

It was an ingenuously disingenuous suggestion; it brought my companion's eyes back to mine, with something of the scorn that I deserved.

"No, Mr. Manders, I meant after what we all heard between Mr. Levy and Mr. Raffles; and you knew very well what I meant," added Miss Belsize severely.

"But surely you didn't take all that seriously?" said I, without denying the just impeachment.

"How could I help it? The insinuation was serious enough, in all conscience!" exclaimed Camilla Belsize.

"That is," said I, since she was not to be wilfully misunderstood, "that poor old Raffles had something to do with this jewel robbery at Carlsbad?"

"If it was a robbery."

She winced at the word.

"Do you mean it might have been a trick?" said I, recalling the victim's own make-believe at the Albany. And not only did Camilla appear to embrace that theory with open arms; she had the nerve to pretend that it really was what she had meant.

"Obviously!" says she, with an impromptu superiority worthy of Raffles himself. "I wonder you never thought of that, Mr. Manders, when you know what a trick you both played Mr. Levy only yesterday. Mr. Raffles himself told us all about that; and I'm very grateful to you both; you must know I am—for Teddy's sake," added Miss Belsize, with one quick remorseful glance towards the great arena. "Still it only shows what Mr. Raffles is—and—and it's what I meant when we were talking about him yesterday."

"I don't remember," said I, remembering fast enough.

"In the rockery," she reminded me. "When you asked what people said about him, and I said that about living on his wits."

"And being a paid amateur!"

"But the other was the worst."

"I'm not so sure," said I. "But his wits wouldn't carry him very far if he only took necklaces and put them back again."

"But it was all a joke," she reminded us both with a bit of a start. "It must have been a joke, if Mr. Raffles did it at all. And it would be dreadful if anything happened to him because of a wretched practical joke!"

There was no mistake about her feeling now; she really felt that it would be "dreadful if anything happened" to the man whom yesterday she had seemed both to dislike and to distrust. Her voice vibrated with anxiety. A bright film covered the fine eyes, and they were finer than ever as they continued to face me unashamed; but I was fool enough to speak my mind, and at that they flashed themselves dry.

"I thought you didn't like him?" had been my remark, and "Who says I do?" was hers. "But he has done a lot for Teddy," she went on, "and never more than yesterday," with her hand for an instant on my arm, "when you helped him! I am dreadfully sorry for Mr. Garland, sorrier than I am for poor Teddy. But Mr. Raffles is more than sorry. I know he means to do what he can. He seems to think there must be something wrong; he spoke of bringing that brute to reason—if not to justice. It would be too dreadful if such a creature could turn the tables on Mr. Raffles by trumping up any charge against him!"

There was an absolute echo of my own tone in "trumping up any charge," and I thought the echo sounded even more insincere. But at least it showed me where we were. Miss Belsize was not deceived; she only wanted me to think she was. Miss Belsize had divined what I knew, but neither of us would admit to the other that the charge against Raffles would be true enough.

"But why should these men follow him?" said I, really wondering why they should. "If there were anything definite against old Raffles, don't you think he would be arrested?"

"Oh! I don't know," was the slightly irritable answer. "I only think he should be warned that he is being followed."

"Whatever he has done?" I ventured.

"Yes!" said she. "Whatever he has done—after what he did for Teddy yesterday!"

"You want me to warn him?"

"Yes—but not from me!"

"And suppose he really did take Mrs. Levy's necklace?"

"That's just what we are supposing."

"But suppose it wasn't for a joke at all?"

I spoke as one playfully plumbing the abysmally absurd; what I did desire to sound was the loyalty of this new, unexpected, and still captious ally. And I thought myself strangely successful at the first cast; for Miss Belsize looked me in the face as I was looking her, and I trusted her before she spoke.

"Well, after yesterday," she said, "I should warn him all the same!"

"You would back your Raffles right or wrong?" I murmured, perceiving that Camilla Belsize was, after all, like all the rest of us.

"Against a vulgar extortioner, most decidedly!" she returned, without repudiating the possessive pronoun. "It doesn't follow that I think anything of him—apart from what you did between you for Teddy yesterday."

We had continued our stroll some time ago, and now it was I who stood still. I looked at my watch. It still wanted some minutes to the luncheon interval.

"If Raffles took a cab to his rooms," I said, "he must be nearly there and I must telephone to him."

"Is there a call-office on the ground?"

"Only in the pavilion, I believe, for the use of the members."

"Then you must go to the nearest one outside."

"And what about you?"

Miss Belsize brightened with her smile of perfect and unconscious independence.

"Oh, I shall be all right," she said. "I know where to find Mr. Garland, even if I don't pick up an escort on the way."

But it was she who escorted me to the tall turnstile nearest Wellington Road.

"And you do see why I want to put Mr. Raffles on his guard?" she said pointedly as we shook hands. "It's only because you and he have done so much for Teddy!"

And because she did not end by reminding me of my promise, I was all the more reluctantly determined to keep it to the letter, even though Raffles should think as ill as ever of one who was at least beginning to think better of him.

XI

A Dash in the Dark

In a few lines which I found waiting for me at the club, and have somewhat imprudently preserved, Raffles professes to have known he was being shadowed even before we met at Lord's: "but it was no use talking about it until the foe were in the cart." He goes on to explain the simple means by which he reduced the gentlemen in billycocks to the pitch of discomfiture implied in his metaphor. He had taken a hansom to the Burlington Gardens entrance to the Albany, and kept it waiting while he went in and changed his clothes; then he had sent Barraclough to pay off the cab, and himself marched out into Piccadilly, what time the billycock brims were still shading watchful eyes in Burlington Gardens. There, to be sure, I myself had spotted one of the precious pair when I drove up after vain exertions at the call-office outside Lord's; but by that time his confederate was on guard at the Piccadilly end, and Raffles had not only shown a clean pair of wings, but left the poor brutes to watch an empty cage. He dismisses them not unfairly with the epithet "amateurish." Thus I was the more surprised, but not the less relieved, to learn that he was "running down into the country for the weekend, to be out of their way"; but he would be back on the Monday night, "to keep an engagement you wot of, Bunny. And if you like you may meet me under the clock at Waterloo (in flannel kit and tennis-shoes for choice) at the witching hour of twelve sharp."

If I liked! I had a premature drink in honour of an invitation more gratifying to my vanity than any compliment old Raffles had paid me yet; for I could still hear his ironical undertaking to let me know if he could not do without me, and there was obviously no irony in this delightfully early intimation of that very flattering fact. It altered my whole view of the case. I might disapprove of the risks Raffles was running for his other friends, but the more I was allowed to share in them the less critical I was inclined to be. Besides I was myself clearly implicated in the issue as between my own friend and the common enemy; it was no more palatable to me than it was to Raffles, to be beaten by Dan Levy after our initial victory over him. So I drank like a man to his destruction, and subsequently stole forth to spy upon his

foolish myrmidons, who flattered themselves that they were spying on Raffles. The imbeciles were at it still! The one hanging about Burlington Gardens looked unutterably bored, but with his blots of whisker and his grimy jowl, as flagrant a detective officer as ever I saw, even if he had not so considerately dressed the part. The other bruiser was an equally distinctive type, with a formidable fighting face and a chest like a barrel; but in Piccadilly he seemed to me less occupied in taking notice than in avoiding it. In innocuous futility one could scarcely excel the other; and between them they raised my spirits to the zenith.

I spent the rest of the afternoon at their own game, dogging Miss Belsize about Lord's until at last I had an opportunity of informing her that Raffles was quite safe. It may be that I made my report with too much gusto when my chance came; at any rate, it was only the fact that appeared to interest Miss Belsize; the details, over which I gloated, seemed to inspire in her a repugnance consistent with the prejudice she had displayed against Raffles yesterday, but not with her grateful solicitude on his behalf as revealed to me that very morning. I could only feel that gratitude was the beginning and the end of her new regard for him. Raffles had never fascinated this young girl as he did the rest of us; ordinarily engaged to an ordinary man, she was proof against the glamour that dazzled us. Nay, though she would not admit it even to me his friend, though like Levy she pretended to embrace the theory of the practical joke, making it the pretext for her anxiety, I felt more certain than ever that she now guessed, and had long suspected, what manner of man Raffles really was, and that her natural antipathy was greater even than before. Still more certain was I that she would never betray him by word or deed; that, whatever harm might come of his present proceedings, it would not be through Camilla Belsize.

But I was now determined to do my own utmost to minimise the dangers, to be a real help to Raffles in the act of altruistic depravity to which he had committed himself, and not merely a fifth wheel to his dashing chariot. Accordingly I went into solemn training for the event before us: a Turkish bath on the Saturday, a quiet Sunday between Mount Street and the club, and most of Monday lying like a log in cold-blooded preparation for the night's work. And when night fell I took it upon me to reconnoitre the ground myself before meeting Raffles at Waterloo.

Another cool and starry evening seemed to have tempted all the town and his wife into the streets. The great streams of traffic were busier

than ever, the backwaters emptier, and Gray's Inn a basin drained to the last dreg of visible humanity. In one moment I passed through gateway and alley from the voices and lights of Holborn into a perfectly deserted square of bare ground and bright stars. The contrast was altogether startling, for I had never been there before; but for the same reason I had already lost my bearings, believing myself to be in Gray's Inn Square when I was only in South Square, Gray's Inn. Here I entered upon a hopeless search for the offices of Burroughs and Burroughs. Door after door had I tried in vain, and was beginning to realise my mistake, when a stray molecule of the population drifted in from Holborn as I had done, but with the quick step of the man who knows his way. I darted from a doorway to inquire mine, but he was across the square before I could cut him off, and as he passed through the rays of a lamp beside a second archway, I fell back thanking Providence and Raffles for my rubber soles. The man had neither seen nor heard me, but at the last moment I had recognised him as the burlier of the two blockheads who had shadowed Raffles three days before.

He passed under the arch without looking round. I flattened myself against the wall on my side of the arch; and in so standing I was all but eye-witness of a sudden encounter in the square beyond.

The quick steps stopped, and there was a "Here you are!" on one side, and a "Well! Where is he?" on the other, both very eager and below the breath.

"On the job," whispered the first voice. "Up to the neck!"

"When did 'e go in?"

"Nearly an hour ago; when I sent the messenger."

"Which way?"

"Up through number seventeen."

"Next door, eh?"

"That's right."

"Over the roof?"

"Can't say; he's left no tracks. I been up to see."

"I suppose there's the usual ladder and trapdoor?"

"Yes, but the ladder's hanging in its proper place. He couldn't have put it back there, could he?"

The other grunted; presently he expressed a doubt whether Raffles (and it thrilled me to hear the very name) had succeeded in breaking into the lawyer's office at all. The first man on the scene, however, was quite sure of it—and so was I.

"And we've got to hang about," grumbled the newcomer, "till he comes out again?"

"That's it. We can't miss him. He must come back into the square or through into the gardens, and if he does that he'll have to come over these here railings into Field Court. We got him either way, and there's a step just here where we can sit and see both ways as though it had been made for us. You come and try. . . a door into the old hall. . ."

That was all I heard distinctly; first their footsteps, and then the few extra yards, made the rest unintelligible. But I had heard enough. "The usual ladder and trap-door!" Those blessed words alone might prove worth their weight in great letters of solid gold.

Now I could breathe again; now I relaxed my body and turned my head, and peered through the arch with impunity, and along the whole western side of Gray's Inn Square, with its dusky fringe of plane-trees and its vivid line of lamps, its strip of pavement, and its wall of many-windowed houses under one unbroken roof. Dim lights smouldered in the column of landing windows over every door; otherwise there was no break in the blackness of that gaunt façade. Yet in some dark room or other behind those walls I seemed to see Raffles at work as plainly as I had just heard our natural enemies plotting his destruction. I saw him at a safe. I saw him at a desk. I saw him leaving everything as he had found it, only to steal down and out into the very arms of the law. And I felt that even that desperate *dénouement* was little more than he deserved for letting me think myself accessory before the fact, when all the time he meant me to have nothing whatever to do with it! Well, I should have everything to do with it now; if Raffles was to be saved from the consequences of his own insanity, I and I alone must save him. It was the chance of my life to show him my real worth. And yet the difficulty of the thing might have daunted Raffles himself.

I knew what to do if only I could gain the house which he had made the base of his own operations; at least I knew what to attempt, and what Raffles had done I might do. So far the wily couple within earshot had helped me out of their own mouths. But they were only just round the corner that hid them from my view; stray words still reached me; and they knew me by sight, would recognise me at a glance, might pounce upon me as I passed. Unless—

I had it!

The crowd in Holborn seemed strange and unreal as I jostled in its midst once more. I was out of it in a moment, however, and into a 'bus, and out of the 'bus in a couple of minutes by my watch. One more minute and I was seeing how far back I could sit in a hansom bound for Gray's Inn Square.

"I forget the number," I had told the cabman, "but it's three or four doors beyond Burroughs and Burroughs, the solicitors."

The gate into Holborn had to be opened for me, but the gate-keeper had not seen me on my previous entrance and exit afoot through the postern. It was when we drove under the further arch into the actual square that I pressed my head hard against the back of the hansom, and turned my face towards Field Court. The enemy might have abandoned their position, they might meet me face to face as I landed on the pavement; that was my risk, and I ran it without disaster. We passed the only house with an outer door to it in the square (now there is none), and on the plate beside it I read BURROUGHS AND BURROUGHS with a thrill. Up went my stick; my shilling (with a peculiarly superfluous sixpence for luck) I thrust through the trap with the other hand; and I was across the pavement, and on the stairs four clear doors beyond the lawyer's office, before the driver had begun to turn his horse.

They were broad bare stairs, with great office doors right and left on every landing, and in the middle the landing window looking out into the square. I waited well within the window on the first floor; and as my hansom drove out under the arch, the light of its near lamp flashed across two figures lounging on the steps of that entrance to the hall; but there was no stopping or challenging the cabman, no sound at all but those of hoofs and bell, and soon only that of my own heart beating as I fled up the rest of the stairs in my rubber soles.

Near the top I paused to thank my kindly stars; sure enough there was a long step-ladder hanging on a great nail over the last half-landing, and a square trap-door right over the landing proper! I ran up just to see the names on the two top doors; one was evidently that of some pettifogging firm of solicitors, while the other bespoke a private resident, whom I judged to be out of town by the congestion of postal matter that met my fingers in his letter-box. Neither had any terrors for me. The step-ladder was unhooked without another moment's hesitation. Care alone was necessary to place it in position without making a noise; then up I went, and up went the trapdoor next, without mishap or hindrance until I tried to stand up in the loft, and caught my head a crack against the tiles instead.

This was disconcerting in more ways than one, for I could not leave the ladder where it was, and it was nearly twice my height. I struck a match and lit up a sufficient perspective of lumber and cobwebs to reassure me. The loft was long enough, and the trap-door plumb under the apex of the roof, whereas I had stepped sideways off the ladder. It was to be got up, and I got it up, though not by any means as silently as I could have wished. I knelt and listened at the open trap-door for a good minute before closing it with great caution, a squeak and a scuttle in the loft itself being the only sign that I had disturbed a living creature.

There was a grimy dormer window, not looking down into the square, but leading like a companion hatchway into a valley of once red tiles, now stained blue-black in the starlight. It was great to stand upright here in the pure night air out of sight of man or beast. Smokeless chimney-stacks deleted whole pages of stars, but put me more in mind of pollards rising out of these rigid valleys, and sprouting with telephone wires that interlaced for foliage. The valley I was in ended fore and aft in a similar slope to that at either side; the length of it doubtless tallied with the frontage of a single house; and when I had clambered over the southern extremity into a precisely similar valley I saw that this must be the case. I had entered the fourth house beyond Burroughs and Burroughs's, or was it the fifth? I threaded three valleys, and then I knew.

In all three there had been dormer windows on either hand, that on the square side leading into the loft; the other, or others, forming a sort of skylight to some top-floor room. Suddenly I struck one of these standing very wide open, and trod upon a rope's end curled like a snake on the leads. I stooped down, and at a touch I knew that I had hold of Raffles's favourite Manila, which united a silken flexibility with the strength of any hawser. It was tied to the window-post, and it dangled into a room in which there was a dull red glow of fire: an inhabited room if ever I put my nose in one! My body must follow, however, where Raffles had led the way; and when it did I came to ground sooner than I expected on something less secure. The dying firelight, struggling through the bars of a kitchen range, showed my tennis-shoes in the middle of the kitchen table. A cat was stretching itself on the hearth-rug as I made a step of a wooden chair, and came down like a cat myself.

I found the kitchen door, found a passage so dark that the window at the end hung like a picture slashed across the middle. Yet it only looked into the square, for I peered out when I had crept along the passage, and even thought I both heard and saw the enemy at their old post. But

I was in another enemy's country now; at every step I stopped to listen for the thud of feet bounding out of bed. Hearing nothing, I had the temerity at last to strike a match upon my trousers, and by its light I found the outer door. This was not bolted nor yet shut; it was merely ajar, and so I left it.

The rooms opposite appeared to be an empty set; those on the second and first floors were only partially shut off by swing doors leading to different departments of the mighty offices of Burroughs and Burroughs. There were no lights upon these landings, and I gathered my information by means of successive matches, whose tell-tale ends I carefully concealed about my person, and from copious legends painted on the walls. Thus I had little difficulty in groping my way to the private offices of Sir John Burroughs, head of the celebrated firm; but I looked in vain for a layer of light under any of the massive mahogany doors with which this portion of the premises was glorified. Then I began softly trying doors that proved to be locked. Only one yielded to my hand; and when it was a few inches open, all was still black; but the next few brought me to the end of my quest, and the close of my solitary adventures.

XII

A Midsummer Night's Work

The dense and total darkness was broken in one place, and one only, by a plateful of light proceeding from a tiny bulb of incandescence in its centre. This blinding atom of white heat lit up a hand hardly moving, a pen continually poised, over a disc of snowy paper; and on the other side, something that lay handy on the table, reflecting the light in its plated parts. It was Raffles at his latest deviltry. He had not heard me, and he could not see; but for that matter he never looked up from his task. Sometimes his face bent over it, and I could watch its absolute concentration. The brow was furrowed, and the mouth pursed, yet there was a hint of the same quiet and wary smile with which Raffles would bowl an over or drill holes in a door.

I stood for some moments fascinated, entranced, before creeping in to warn him of my presence in a whisper. But this time he heard my step, snatched up electric torch and glittering revolver, and covered me with the one in the other's light.

"A.J.!" I gasped.

"Bunny!" he exclaimed in equal amazement and displeasure. "What the devil do you mean by this?"

"You're in danger," I whispered. "I came to warn you!"

"Danger? I'm never out of it. But how did you know where to find me, and how on God's earth did *you* get here?"

"I'll tell you some other time. You know those two brutes you dodged the other day?"

"I ought to."

"They're waiting below for you at this very moment."

Raffles peered a few moments through the handful of white light between our faces.

"Let them wait!" said he, and replaced the torch upon the table and put down his revolver for his pen.

"They're detectives!" I urged.

"Are they, Bunny?"

"What else could they be?"

"What, indeed!" murmured Raffles, as he fell to work again with bent head and deliberate pen.

"You gave them the slip on Friday, but they must have known your game and lain in wait for you here, one or other of them, ever since. It's my belief Dan Levy put them up to it, and the yarn about the letter was just to tempt you into this trap and get you caught in the act. He didn't want a copy one bit; for God's sake, don't stop to finish it now!"

"I don't agree with you," said Raffles without looking up, "and I don't do things by halves, Your precious detectives must have patience, Bunny, and so must you." He held his watch to the bulb. "In about twenty minutes there'll be real danger, but we couldn't be safer in our beds for the next ten. So perhaps you'll let me finish without further interruption, or else get out by yourself as you came in."

I turned away from Raffles and his light, and blundered back to the landing. The blood boiled in my veins. Here had I fought and groped my way to his side, through difficulties it might have taxed even him to surmount, as one man swims ashore with a rope from the wreck, at the same mortal risk, with the same humane purpose. And not a word of thanks, not one syllable of congratulation, but "get out by yourself as you came in!" I had more than half a mind to get out, and for good; nay, as I stood and listened on the landing, I could have found it in my outraged heart to welcome those very sleuthhounds from the square, with a cordon of police behind them.

Yet my boiling blood ran cold when warm breath smote my cheek and a hand my shoulder at one and the same awful moment.

"Raffles!" I cried in a strangled voice.

"Hush, Bunny!" he chuckled in my ear. "Didn't you know who it was?"

"I never heard you; why did you steal on me like that?"

"You see you're not the only one who can do it, Bunny! I own it would have served me right if you'd brought the square about our ears."

"Have you finished in there?" I asked gruffly.

"Rather!"

"Then you'd better hurry up and put everything as you found it."

"It's all done, Bunny; red tape tied on such a perfect forgery that the crux will be to prove it is one; safe locked up, and every paper in its place."

"I never heard a sound."

"I never made one," said Raffles, leading me upstairs by the arm. "You see how you put me on my mettle, Bunny, old boy!"

I said no more till we reached the self-contained flat at the top of the house; then I begged Raffles to be quiet in a lower whisper than his own.

"Why, Bunny? Do you think there are people inside?"

"Aren't there?" I cried aloud in my relief.

"You flatter me, Bunny!" laughed Raffles, as we groped our way in. "This is where they keep their John Bulldog, a magnificent figure of a commissionaire with the V.C. itself on his manly bosom. Catch me come when he was at home; one of us would have had to die, and it would have been a shame either way. Poor pussy, then, poor puss!"

We had reached the kitchen and the cat was rubbing itself against Raffles's legs.

"But how on earth did you get rid of him for the night?"

"Made friends with him when I called on Friday; didn't I tell you I had an appointment with the bloated head of this notorious firm when I cleared out of Lord's? I'm about to strengthen his already unrivalled list of clients; you shall hear all about that later. We had another interview this afternoon, when I asked my V.C. if he ever went to the theatre; you see he had spotted Tom Fool, and told me he never had a chance of getting to Lord's. So I got him tickets for 'Rosemary' instead, but of course I swore they had just been given to me and I couldn't use them. You should have seen how the hero beamed! So that's where he is, he and his wife—or was, until the curtain went down."

"Good Lord, Raffles, is the piece over?"

"Nearly ten minutes ago, but it'll take 'em all that unless they come home in a cab."

And Raffles had been sitting before the fire, on the kitchen table, encouraging the cat, when this formidable V.C. and his wife must be coming every instant nearer Gray's Inn Square!

"Why, my dear Bunny, I should back myself to swarm up and out without making a sound or leaving a sign, if I heard our hero's key in the lock this moment. After you, Bunny."

I climbed up with trembling knees, Raffles holding the rope taut to make it easier. Once more I stood upright under the stars and the telephone wires, and leaned against a chimney-stack to wait for Raffles. But before I saw him, before I even heard his unnecessarily noiseless movements, I heard something else that sent a chill all through me.

It was not the sound of a key in the lock. It was something far worse than that. It was the sound of voices on the roof, and of footsteps drawing nearer through the very next valley of leads and tiles.

I was crouching on the leads outside the dormer window as Raffles climbed into sight within.

"They're after us up here!" I whispered in his face. "On the next roof! I hear them!"

Up came Raffles with his hands upon the sill, then with his knees between his hands, and so out on all-fours into the narrow rivulet of lead between the sloping tiles. Out of the opposite slope, a yard or two on, rose a stout stack of masonry, a many-headed monster with a chimney-pot on each, and a full supply of wires for whiskers. Behind this Gorgon of the house-tops Raffles hustled me without a word, and himself took shelter as the muffled voices on the next roof grew more distinct. They were the voices that I had overheard already in the square, the voices but not the tones. The tones—the words—were those of an enemy divided against itself.

"And now we've gone and come too far!" grumbled the one who had been last to arrive upon the scene below.

"We did that," the other muttered, "the moment we came in after 'em. We should've stopped where we were."

"With that other cove driving up and going in without ever showing a glim?"

Raffles nudged me, and I saw what I had done. But the weakling of the pair still defended the position he had reluctantly abandoned on *terra firma*; he was all for returning while there was time; and there were fragments of the broken argument that were beginning to puzzle me when a soft oath from the man in front proclaimed the discovery of the open window and the rope.

"We got 'em," he whispered, stagily, "like rats in a trap!"

"You forget what it is we've got to get."

"Well, we must first catch our man, mustn't we? And how d'ye know his pal hasn't gone in to warn him where we were? If he has, and we'd stopped there, they'd do us easy."

"They may do us easier down there in the dark," replied the other, with a palpable shiver. "They'll hear us and lie in wait. In the dark! We shan't have a dog's chance."

"All right! You get out of it and save your skin. I'd rather work alone than with a blessed funk!"

The situation was identical with many a one in the past between Raffles and me. The poor brute in my part resented the charge against his courage as warmly as I had always done. He was merely for the better part of valour, and how right he was Raffles and I only knew. I hoped the lesson was not lost upon Raffles. Dialogue and action alike resembled one of our own performances far more than ordinary police methods as we knew them. We heard the squeeze of the leader's clothes and the rattle of his buttons over the window ledge. "It's like old times," we heard him mutter; and before many moments the weakling was impulsively whispering down to know if he should follow.

I felt for that fellow at every stage of his unwilling proceedings. I was to feel for him still more. Raffles had stepped down like a cat from behind our cover; grasping an angle of the stack with either hand, I put my head round after him. The wretched player of my old part was on his haunches at the window, stooping forward, more in than out. I saw Raffles grinning in the starlight, saw his foot poised and the other poor devil disappear. Then a dull bump, then a double crash and such a cursing as left no doubt that the second fellow had fallen plumb on top of the first. Also from his language I fancied he would survive the fall.

But Raffles took no peep at his handiwork; hardly had the rope whipped out at my feet than he had untied the other end.

"Like lamplighters, Bunny!"

And back we went helter-skelter along the valleys of lead and over the hills of tile. . . The noise in the kitchen died away as we put a roof or two between us and that of Burroughs and Burroughs.

"This is where I came out," I called to Raffles as he passed the place. "There's a ladder here where I left it in the loft!"

"No time for ladders!" cried Raffles over his shoulder, and not for some moments did he stop in his stride. Nor was it I who stopped him then; it was a sudden hubbub somewhere behind us, somewhere below; the blowing of a police whistle, and the sound of many footsteps in the square.

"That's for us!" I gasped. "The ladder! The ladder!"

"Ladder be damned!" returned Raffles, roughly. "It isn't for us at all; it's my pal the V.C. who has come home and bottled the other blighters."

"Thinking they're thieves?"

"Thinking any rot you like! Our course is over the rest of the roofs on this side, over the whole lot at the top end, and, if possible, down the last staircase in the corner. Then we only have to show ourselves in the square for a tick before we're out by way of Verulam Buildings."

"Is there another gate there?" I asked as he scampered on with me after him.

"Yes; but it's closed and the porter leaves at twelve, and it must be jolly near that now. Wait, Bunny! Some one or other is sure to be looking out of the top windows across the square; they'll see us if we take our fences too freely!"

We had come to one of the transverse tile-slopes, which hitherto we had run boldly up and down in our helpful and noiseless rubber soles; now, not to show ourselves against the stars, to a stray pair of eyes on some other high level, we crept up on all fours and rolled over at full length. It added considerably to our time over more than a whole side of the square. Meanwhile the police whistles had stopped, but the company in the square had swollen audibly.

It seemed an age, but I suppose it was not many minutes, before we came to the last of the dormer windows, looking into the last vale of tiles in the north-east angle of the square. Something gleamed in the starlight, there was a sharp little sound of splitting wood, and Raffles led me on hands and knees into just such a loft as I had entered before by ladder. His electric torch discovered the trapdoor at a gleam. Raffles opened it and let down the rope, only to whisk it up again so smartly that it struck my face like a whiplash.

A door had opened on the top landing. We listened over the open trap-door, and knew that another stood listening on the invisible threshold underneath; then we saw him running downstairs, and my heart leapt for he never once looked up. I can see him still, foreshortened by our bird's-eye view into a Turkish fez and a fringe of white hair and red neck, a billow of dressing-gown, and bare heels peeping out of bedroom slippers at every step that we could follow; but no face all the way down, because he was a bent old boy who never looked like looking up.

Raffles threw his rope aside, gave me his hand instead, and dropped me on the landing like a feather, dropping after me without a moment's pause. In fact, the old fellow with the fez could hardly have completed his descent of the stairs when we began ours. Yet through the landing window we saw him charging diagonally across the square, shouting and gesticulating in his flight to the gathering crowd near the far corner.

"He spotted us, Bunny!" exclaimed Raffles, after listening an instant in the entrance. "Stick to me like my shadow, and do every blessed thing I do."

Out he dived, I after him, and round to the left with the speed of lightning, but apparently not without the lightning's attribute of attracting attention to itself. There was a hullabaloo across the square behind us, and I looked round to see the crowd there breaking in our direction, as I rushed after Raffles under an arch and up the alley in front of Verulam Buildings.

It was striking midnight as we made our sprint along this alley, and at the far end the porter was preparing to depart, but he waited to let us through the gate into Gray's Inn Road, and not until he had done so can the hounds have entered the straight. We did not hear them till the gate had clanged behind us, nor had it opened again before we were high and dry in a hansom.

"King's Cross!" roared Raffles for all the street to hear; but before we reached Clerkenwell Road he said he meant Waterloo, and round we went to the right along the tram-lines. I was too breathless to ask questions, and Raffles offered no explanations until he had lit a Sullivan. "That little bit of wrong way may lose us our train," he said as he puffed the first cloud. "But it'll shoot the whole field to King's Cross as sure as scent is scent; and if we do catch our train, Bunny, we shall have it to ourselves as far as this pack is concerned. Hurrah! Blackfriar's Bridge and a good five minutes to go!"

"You're going straight down to Levy's with the letter?"

"Yes; that's why I wanted you to meet me under the clock at twelve."

"But why in tennis-shoes?" I asked, recalling the injunctions in his note, and the meaning that I had naturally read into them.

"I thought we might possibly finish the night on the river," replied Raffles, darkly. "I think so still."

"And *I* thought you meant me to lend you a hand in Gray's Inn!"

Raffles laughed.

"The less you think, my dear old Bunny, the better it always is! To-night, for example, you have performed prodigies on my account; your unselfish audacity has only been equalled by your resource; but, my dear fellow, it was a sadly unnecessary effort."

"Unnecessary to tell you those brutes were waiting for you down below?"

"Quite, Bunny. I saw one of them and let him see me. I knew he'd send off for his pal."

"Then I don't understand your tactics or theirs."

"Mine were to walk out the very way we did, you and I. They would never have seen me from the opposite corner of the square, or dreamt of going in after me if they hadn't spotted your getting in before them to put me on my guard. The place would have been left exactly as I found it, and those two numskulls as much in the lurch as I left them last week outside the Albany."

"Perhaps they were beginning to fear that," said I, "and meant ferreting for you in any case if you didn't show up."

"Not they," said Raffles. "One of them was against it as it was; it wasn't their job at all."

"Not to take you in the act if they could?"

"No; their job was to take the letter from me as soon as I got back to earth. That was all. I happen to know. Those were their instructions from old Levy."

"Levy!"

"Did it never occur to you that I was being dogged by his creatures?"

"His creatures, Raffles?"

"He set them to shadow me from the hour of our interview on Saturday morning. Their instructions were to bag the letter from me as soon as I got it, but to let me go free to the devil!"

"How can you know, A.J.?"

"My dear Bunny, where do you suppose I've been spending the week-end? Did you think I'd go in with a sly dog like old Shylock without watching him and finding out his real game? I should have thought it hardly necessary to tell you I've been down the river all the time; down the river," added Raffles, chuckling, "in a Canadian canoe and a torpedo beard! I was cruising near the foot of the old brute's garden on Friday evening when one of the precious pair came down to tell him they had let me slip already. I landed and heard the whole thing through the window of the room where we shall find him to-night. It was Levy who set them to watch the crib since they'd lost the cracksman; he was good enough to reiterate all his orders for my benefit. You will hear me take him through them when we get down there, so it's no use going over the same ground twice."

"Funny orders for a couple of Scotland Yard detectives!" was my puzzled comment as Raffles produced an inordinate cab-fare.

"Scotland Yard?" said he. "My good Bunny, those were no limbs of the law; they're old thieves set to catch a thief, and they've been caught themselves for their pains!"

Of course they were! Every detail of their appearance and their behaviour confirmed the statement in the flash that brought them all before my mind! And I had never thought of it, never but dreamt that we were doing battle with the archenemies of our class. But there was no time for further reflection, nor had I recovered breath enough for another word, when the hansom clattered up the cobbles into Waterloo Station. And our last sprint of that athletic night ended in a simultaneous leap into separate carriages as the platform slid away from the 12:10 train.

XIII

Knocked Out

B ut it was hardly likely to be the last excitement of the night, as I saw for myself before Raffles joined me at Vauxhall. An archtraitor like Daniel Levy might at least be trusted to play the game out with loaded dice; no single sportsman could compete against his callous machinations; and that was obviously where I was coming in. I only wished I had not come in before! I saw now the harm that I had done by my rash proceedings in Gray's Inn, the extra risk entailed already and a worse one still impending. If the wretches who had shadowed him were really Levy's mercenaries, and if they really had been taken in their own trap, their first measure of self-defence would be the denunciation of Raffles to the real police. Such at least was my idea, and Raffles himself made light enough of it; he thought they could not expose him without dragging in Levy, who had probably made it worth their while not to do that on any consideration. His magnanimity in the matter, which he flatly refused to take as seriously as I did, made it difficult for me to press old Raffles, as I otherwise might have done, for an outline of those further plans in which I hoped to atone for my blunders by being of some use to him after all. His nonchalant manner convinced me that they were cut-and-dried; but I was left perhaps deservedly in the dark as to the details. I merely gathered that he had brought down some document for Levy to sign in execution of the verbal agreement made between them in town; not until that agreement was completed by his signature was the harpy to receive the precious epistle he pretended never to have written. Raffles, in fine, had the air of a man who has the game in his hands, who is none the less prepared for foul play on the other side, and by no means perturbed at the prospect.

We left the train at a sweet-smelling platform, on which the lights were being extinguished as we turned into a quiet road where bats flew over our heads between the lamp-posts, and a policeman was passing a disc of light over a jerry-built abuse of the name of Queen Anne. Our way led through quieter roads of larger houses standing further back, until at last we came to the enemy's gates. They were wooden gates without a lodge, yet the house set well beyond them, on the river's brim, was a mansion of considerable size and still greater peculiarity. It was really two houses, large and small, connected by a spine of white posts and joists and glimmering glass. In the more substantial building no lights were to be seen from the gates, but in the annex a large French window made a lighted square at right angles with the river and the road. We had set foot in the gravel drive; with a long line of poplars down one side, and on the other a wide lawn dotted with cedars and small shrubs, when Raffles strode among these with a smothered exclamation, and a wild figure started from the ground.

"What are you doing here?" demanded Raffles, with all the righteous austerity of a law-abiding citizen.

"Nutting, sare!" replied an alien tongue, a gleam of good teeth in the shadow of his great soft hat. "I been see Mistare Le-vie in ze 'ouse, on ze beezness, shentlemen."

"Seen him, have you? Then if I were you I should make a decent departure," said Raffles, "by the gate—" to which he pointed with increased severity of tone and bearing.

The weird figure uncovered a shaggy head of hair, made us a grotesque bow with his right hand melodramatically buried in the folds of a voluminous cape, and stalked off in the starlight with much dignity. But we heard him running in the road before the gate had clicked behind him.

"Isn't that the fellow we saw in Jermyn Street last Thursday?" I asked Raffles in a whisper.

"That's the chap," he whispered back. "I wonder if he spotted us, Bunny? Levy's treated him scandalously, of course; it all came out in a torrent the other morning. I only hope he hasn't been serving Dan Levy as Jack Rutter served old Baird! I could swear that was a weapon of sorts he'd got under his cloak."

And as we stood together under the stars, listening to the last of the runaway footfalls, I recalled the killing of another and a less notorious usurer by a man we both knew, and had even helped to shield from the consequences of his crime. Yet the memory of our terrible discovery on that occasion had not the effect of making me shrink from such another now; nor could I echo the hope of Raffles in my heart of hearts. If Dan Levy also had come to a bad end—well, it was no more than he deserved, if only for his treachery to Raffles, and, at any rate, it would put a stop to our plunging from bad to worse in an adventure of which the sequel might well be worst of all. I do not say that I was wicked enough absolutely to desire the death of this sinner for our benefit; but I saw the benefit at least as plainly as the awful possibility, and it was not with unalloyed relief that I beheld a great figure stride through the lighted windows at our nearer approach.

Though his back was to the light before I saw his face, and the whole man might have been hacked out of ebony, it was every inch the living Levy who stood peering in our direction, one hand hollowed at an ear, the other shading both eyes.

"Is that you, boys?" he croaked in sepulchral salute.

"It depends which boys you mean," replied Raffles, marching into the zone of light. "There are so many of us about to-night!"

Levy's arms dropped at his sides, and I heard him mutter "Raffles!" with a malediction. Next moment he was inquiring whether we had come down alone, yet peering past us into the velvet night for his answer.

"I brought our friend Bunny," said Raffles, "but that's all."

"Then what do you mean by saying there are so many of you about?"

"I was thinking of the gentleman who was here just before us."

"Here just before you? Why, I haven't seen a soul since my 'ousehold went to bed."

"But we met the fellow just this minute within your gates: a little foreign devil with a head like a mop and the cloak of an operatic conspirator."

"That beggar!" cried Levy, flying into a high state of excitement on the spot. "That blessed little beggar on my tracks down here! I've 'ad him thrown out of the office in Jermyn Street; he's threatened me by letter and telegram; so now he thinks he'll come and try it on in person down 'ere. Seen me, eh? I wish I'd seen '*im*! I'm ready for biters like that, gentlemen. I'm not to be caught on the 'op down here!"

And a plated revolver twinkled and flashed in the electric light as Levy drew it from his hip pocket and flourished it in our faces; he would have gone prowling through the grounds with it if Raffles had not assured him that the foreign foe had fled on our arrival. As it was the pistol was not put back in his pocket when Levy at length conducted us indoors; he placed it on an occasional table beside the glass that he drained on entering; and forthwith set his back to a fire which seemed in keeping with the advanced hour, and doubly welcome in an apartment so vast that the billiard table was a mere item at one end, and sundry trophies of travel and the chase a far more striking and unforeseen feature.

"Why, that's a better grisly than the one at Lord's!" exclaimed Raffles, pausing to admire a glorious fellow near the door, while I mixed myself the drink he had declined.

"Yes," said Levy, "the man that shot all this lot used to go about saying he'd shoot *me* at one time; but I need 'ardly tell you he gave it up as a bad job, and went an' did what some folks call a worse instead. He didn't get much show 'ere, *I* can tell you; that little foreign snipe won't either, nor yet any other carrion that think they want my blood. I'd empty this shooter o' mine into their in'ards as soon as look at 'em, I don't give a curse who they are! Just as well I wasn't brought up to your profession, eh, Raffles?"

"I don't quite follow you, Mr. Levy."

"Oh yes you do!" said the money-lender, with his gastric chuckle. "How've you got on with that little bit o' burgling?"

And I saw him screw up his bright eyes, and glance through the open windows into the outer darkness, as though there was still a hope in his mind that we had not come down alone. I formed the impression that Levy had returned by a fairly late train himself, for he was in morning dress, in dusty boots, and there was an abundant supply of sandwiches on the table with the drinks. But he seemed to have confined his own attentions to the bottle, and I liked to think that the sandwiches had been cut for the two emissaries for whom he was welcome to look out for all night.

"How did you get on?" he repeated when he had given them up for the present.

"For a first attempt," replied Raffles, without a twinkle, "I don't think I've done so badly."

"Ah! I keep forgetting you're a young beginner," said Levy, catching the old note in his turn.

"A beginner who's scarcely likely to go on, Mr. Levy, if all cribs are as easy to crack as that lawyers' office of yours in Gray's Inn Square."

"As easy?"

Raffles recollected his pose.

"It was enormous fun," said he. "Of course one couldn't know that there would be no hitch. There was an exciting moment towards the end. I have to thank you for quite a new thrill of sorts. But, my dear Mr. Levy, it was as easy as ringing the bell and being shown in; it only took rather longer."

"What about the caretaker?" asked the usurer, with a curiosity no longer to be concealed.

"He obliged me by taking his wife to the theatre."

"At your expense?"

"No, Mr. Levy, the item will be debited to you in due course."

"So you got in without any difficulty?"

"Over the roof."

"And then?"

"I hit upon the right room."

"And then, Raffles?"

"I opened the right safe."

"Go on, man!"

But the man was only going on at his own rate, and the more Levy pressed him, the greater his apparent reluctance to go on at all.

"Well, I found the letter all right. Oh, yes, I made a copy of it. Was it a good copy? Almost too good, if you ask me." Thus Raffles under increasing pressure.

"Well? Well? You left that one there, I suppose? What happened next?"

There was no longer any masking the moneylender's eagerness to extract the *dénouement* of Raffles's adventure; that it required extracting must have seemed a sufficient earnest of the ultimate misadventure so craftily plotted by Levy himself. His great nose glowed with the imminence of victory. His strong lips loosened their habitual hold upon each other, and there was an impressionist daub of yellow fang between. The brilliant little eyes were reduced to sparkling pinheads of malevolent glee. This was not the fighting face I knew better and despised less, it was the living epitome of low cunning and foul play.

"The next thing that happened," said Raffles, in his most leisurely manner, "was the descent of Bunny like a bolt from the blue."

"Had he gone in with you?"

"No; he came in after me as bold as blazes to say that a couple of common, low detectives were waiting for me down below in the square!"

"That was very kind of 'im," snarled Levy, pouring a murderous fire upon my person from his little black eyes.

"Kind!" cried Raffles. "It saved the whole show."

"It did, did it?"

"I had time to dodge the limbs of the law by getting out another way, and never letting them know that I had got out at all."

"Then you left them there?"

"In their glory!" said Raffles, radiant in his own.

Though I must confess I could not see them at the time, there were excellent reasons for not stating there and then the delicious plight in which we had really left Levy's myrmidons. I myself would have driven home our triumph and his treachery by throwing our winning cards upon the table and simultaneously exposing his false play. But Raffles was right, and I should have been wrong, as I was soon enough to see for myself.

"And you came away, I suppose," suggested the money-lender, ironically, "with my original letter in your pocket?"

"Oh, no, I didn't," replied Raffles, with a reproving shake of the head.

"I thought not!" cried Levy in a gust of exultation.

"I came away," said Raffles, "if you'll pardon the correction, with the letter you never dreamt of writing, Mr. Levy!"

The Jew turned a deeper shade of yellow; but he had the wisdom and the self-control otherwise to ignore the point against him. "You'd better let me see it," said he, and flung out his open hand with a gesture of authority which it took a Raffles to resist.

Levy was still standing with his back to the fire, and I was at his feet in a saddle-bag chair, with my yellow beaker on the table at my elbow. But Raffles remained aloof upon his legs, and he withdrew still further from the fire as he unfolded a large sheet of office paper, stamped with the notorious address in Jermyn Street, and displayed it on high like a phylactery.

"You may see, by all means, Mr. Levy," said Raffles, with a slight but sufficient emphasis on his verb.

"But I'm not to touch—is that it?"

"I'm afraid I must ask you to look first," said Raffles, smiling. "I should suggest, however, that you exercise the same caution in showing me that part of your *quid pro quo* which you have doubtless in readiness; the other part is in my pocket ready for you to sign; and after that, the three little papers can change hands simultaneously."

Nothing could have excelled the firmness of this intimation, except the exggravating delicacy with which it was conveyed. I saw Levy clench and unclench his great fists, and his canine jaw working protuberantly as he ground his teeth. But not a word escaped him, and I was admiring the monster's self-control when of a sudden he swooped upon the table at my side, completely filled his empty glass with neat whiskey, and, spluttering and blinking from an enormous gulp, made a lurch for Raffles with his drink in one hand and his plated pistol in the other.

"Now I'll have a look," he hiccoughed, "an' a good look, unless you want a lump of lead in your liver!"

Raffles awaited his uncertain advance with a contemptuous smile.

"You're not such a fool as all that, Mr. Levy, drunk or sober," said he; but his eye was on the waving weapon, and so was mine; and I was wondering how a man could have got so very suddenly drunk, when the nobbler of crude spirit was hurled with most sober aim, glass and all, full in the face of Raffles, and the letter plucked from his grasp and flung upon the fire, while Raffles was still reeling in his blindness, and before I had struggled to my feet.

Raffles, for the moment, was absolutely blinded; as I say, his face was streaming with blood and whiskey, and the prince of traitors already crowing over his vile handiwork. But that was only for a moment, too; the blackguard had been fool enough to turn his back on me; and, first jumping upon my chair, I sprang upon him like any leopard, and brought him down with my ten fingers in his neck, and such a crack on the parquet with his skull as left it a deadweight on my hands. I remember the rasping of his bristles as I disengaged my fingers and let the leaden head fall back; it fell sideways now, and if it had but looked less dead I believe I should have stamped the life out of the reptile on the spot.

I know that I rose exultant from my deed. . .

XIV

Corpus Delicti

Raffles was still stamping and staggering with his knuckles in his eyes, and I heard him saying, "The letter, Bunny, the letter!" in a way that made me realise all at once that he had been saying nothing else since the moment of the foul assault. It was too late now and must have been from the first; a few filmy scraps of blackened paper, stirring on the hearth, were all that remained of the letter by which Levy had set such store, for which Raffles had risked so much.

"He's burnt it," said I. "He was too quick for me."

"And he's nearly burnt my eyes out," returned Raffles, rubbing them again. "He was too quick for us both."

"Not altogether," said I, grimly. "I believe I've cracked his skull and finished him off!"

Raffles rubbed and rubbed until his bloodshot eyes were blinking out of a blood-stained face into that of the fallen man. He found and felt the pulse in a wrist like a ship's cable.

"No, Bunny, there's some life in him yet! Run out and see if there are any lights in the other part of the house."

When I came back Raffles was listening at the door leading into the long glass passage.

"Not a light!" said I.

"Nor a sound," he whispered. "We're in better luck than we might have been; even his revolver didn't go off." Raffles extracted it from under the prostrate body. "It might just as easily have gone off and shot him, or one of us." And he put the pistol in his own pocket.

"But have I killed him, Raffles?"

"Not yet, Bunny."

"But do you think he's going to die?"

I was overcome by reaction now; my knees knocked together, my teeth chattered in my head; nor could I look any longer upon the great body sprawling prone, or the insensate head twisted sideways on the parquet floor.

"He's all right," said Raffles, when he had knelt and felt and listened again. I whimpered a pious but inconsistent ejaculation. Raffles sat back on his heels, and meditatively wiped a smear of his own blood from the polished floor. "You'd better leave him to me," he said, looking and getting up with sudden decision.

"But what am I to do?"

"Go down to the boathouse and wait in the boat."

"Where is the boathouse?"

"You can't miss it if you follow the lawn down to the water's edge. There's a door on this side; if it isn't open, force it with this."

And he passed me his pocket jimmy as naturally as another would have handed over a bunch of keys.

"And what then?"

"You'll find yourself on the top step leading down to the water; stand tight, and lash out all round until you find a windlass. Wind that windlass as gingerly as though it were a watch with a weak heart; you will be raising a kind of portcullis at the other end of the boathouse, but if you're heard doing it at dead of night we may have to run or swim for it. Raise the thing just high enough to let us under in the boat, and then lie low on board till I come."

Reluctant to leave that ghastly form upon the floor, but now stricken helpless in its presence, I was softer wax than ever in the hands of Raffles, and soon found myself alone in the dew upon an errand in which I neither saw nor sought for any point. Enough that Raffles had given me something to do for our salvation; what part he had assigned to himself, what he was about indoors already, and the nature of his ultimate design, were questions quite beyond me for the moment. I did not worry about them. Had I killed my man? That was the one thing that mattered to me, and I frankly doubt whether even it mattered at the time so supremely as it seemed to have mattered now. Away from the *corpus delicti*, my horror was already less of the deed than of the consequences, and I had quite a level view of those. What I had done was barely even manslaughter at the worst. But at the best the man was not dead. Raffles was bringing him to life again. Alive or dead, I could trust him to Raffles, and go about my own part of the business, as indeed I did in a kind of torpor of the normal sensibilities.

Not much do I remember of that dreamy interval, until the dream became the nightmare that was still in store. The river ran like a broad road under the stars, with hardly a glimmer and not a floating thing upon it. The boathouse stood at the foot of a file of poplars, and I only found it by stooping low and getting everything over my own height against the stars. The door was not locked; but the darkness within was such that I could not see my own hand as it wound the windlass inch by inch. Between the slow ticking of the cogs I listened jealously for foreign sounds, and heard at length a gentle dripping across the breadth of the boathouse; that was the last of the "portcullis," as Raffles called it, rising out of the river; indeed, I could now see the difference in the stretch of stream underneath, for the open end of the boathouse was much less dark than mine; and when the faint band of reflected starlight had broadened as I thought enough, I ceased winding and groped my way down the steps into the boat.

But inaction at such a crisis was an intolerable state, and the last thing I wanted was time to think. With nothing more to do I must needs wonder what I was doing in the boat, and then what Raffles could want with the boat if it was true that Levy was not seriously hurt. I could see the strategic value of my position if we had been robbing the house, but Raffles was not out for robbery this time; and I did not believe he would suddenly change his mind. Could it be that he had never been quite confident of the recovery of Levy, but had sent me to prepare this means of escape from the scene of a tragedy? I cannot have been long in the boat, for my thwart was still rocking under me, when this suspicion shot me ashore in a cold sweat. In my haste I went into the river up to one knee, and ran across the lawn with that boot squelching. Raffles came out of the lighted room to meet me, and as he stood like Levy against the electric glare, the first thing I noticed was that he was wearing an overcoat that did not belong to him, and that the pockets of this overcoat were bulging grotesquely. But it was the last thing I remembered in the horror that was to come.

Levy was lying where I had left him, only straighter, and with a cushion under his head, as though he were not merely dead, but laid out in his clothes where he had fallen.

"I was just coming for you, Bunny," whispered Raffles before I could find my voice. "I want you to take hold of his boots."

"His boots!" I gasped, taking Raffles by the sleeve instead. "What on earth for?"

"To carry him down to the boat!"

"But is he—is he still—"

"Alive?" Raffles was smiling as though I amused him mightily. "Rather, Bunny! Too full of life to be left, I can tell you; but it'll be daylight if we stop for explanations now. Are you going to lend a hand, or am I to drag him through the dew myself?"

I lent every fibre, and Raffles raised the lifeless trunk, I suppose by the armpits, and led the way backward into the night, after switching off the lights within. But the first stage of our revolting journey was a very short one. We deposited our poor burden as charily as possible on the gravel, and I watched over it for some of the longest minutes of my life, while Raffles shut and fastened all the windows, left the room as Levy himself might have left it, and finally found his way out by one of the doors. And all the while not a movement or a sound came from the senseless clay at my feet; but once, when I bent over him, the smell of whiskey was curiously vital and reassuring.

We started off again, Raffles with every muscle on the strain, I with every nerve; this we staggered across the lawn without a rest, but at the boathouse we put him down in the dew, until I took off my coat and we got him lying on that while we debated about the boathouse, its darkness, and its steps. The combination beat us on a moment's consideration; and again I was the one to stay, and watch, and listen to my own heart beating; and then to the water bubbling at the prow and dripping from the blades as Raffles sculled round to the edge of the lawn.

I need dwell no more upon the difficulty and the horror of getting that inanimate mass on board; both were bad enough, but candour compels me to admit that the difficulty dwarfed all else until at last we overcame it. How near we were to swamping our craft, and making sure of our victim by drowning, I still shudder to remember; but I think it must have prevented me from shuddering over more remote possibilities at the time. It was a time, if ever there was one, to trust in Raffles and keep one's powder dry; and to that extent I may say I played the game. But it was his game, not mine, and its very object was unknown to me. Never, in fact, had I followed my inveterate leader quite so implicitly, so blindly, or with such reckless excitement. And yet, if the worst did happen and our mute passenger was never to open his eyes again, it seemed to me that we were well on the road to turn manslaughter into murder in the eyes of any British jury: the road that might easily lead to destruction at the hangman's hands.

But a more immediate menace seemed only to have awaited the actual moment of embarkation, when, as we were pushing off, the rhythmical plash and swish of a paddle fell suddenly upon our ears, and we clutched the bank while a canoe shot down-stream within a length of us. Luckily the night was as dark as ever, and all we saw of the paddler was a white shirt fluttering as it passed. But there lay Levy with his heavy head between my shins in the stern-sheets, with his waistcoat open, and *his* white shirt catching what light there was as greedily as the other; and his white face as conspicuous to my guilty mind as though we had rubbed it with phosphorus. Nor was I the only one to lay this last peril to heart. Raffles sat silent for several minutes on his thwart; and when he did dip his sculls it was to muffle his strokes so that even I could scarcely hear them, and to keep peering behind him down the Stygian stream.

So long had we been getting under way that nothing surprised me more than the extreme brevity of our actual voyage. Not many houses and gardens had slipped behind us on the Middlesex shore, when we turned into an inlet running under the very windows of a house so near the river itself that even I might have thrown a stone from any one of them into Surrey. The inlet was empty and ill-smelling; there was a crazy landing-stage, and the many windows overlooking us had the black gloss of empty darkness within. Seen by starlight with a troubled eye, the house had one salient feature in the shape of a square tower, which stood out from the facade fronting the river, and rose to nearly twice the height of the main roof. But this curious excrescence only added to the forbidding character of as gloomy a mansion as one could wish to approach by stealth at dead of night.

"What's this place?" I whispered as Raffles made fast to a post.

"An unoccupied house, Bunny."

"Do you mean to occupy it?"

"I mean our passenger to do so—if we can land him alive or dead!"

"Hush, Raffles!"

"It's a case of heels first, this time—"

"Shut up!"

Raffles was kneeling on the landing-stage—luckily on a level with our rowlocks—and reaching down into the boat.

"Give me his heels," he muttered; "you can look after his business end. You needn't be afraid of waking the old hound, nor yet hurting him."

"I'm not," I whispered, though mere words had never made my blood run colder. "You don't understand me. Listen to that!"

And as Raffles knelt on the landing-stage, and I crouched in the boat, with something desperately like a dead man stretched between us, there was a swish and a dip outside the inlet, and a flutter of white on the river beyond.

"Another narrow squeak!" he muttered with grim levity when the sound had died away. "I wonder who it is paddling his own canoe at dead of night?"

"I'm wondering how much he saw."

"Nothing," said Raffles, as though there could be no two opinions on the point. "What did we see to swear to between a sweater and a pocket-handkerchief? Only something white, and we were looking out, and it's far darker in here than out there on the main stream. But it'll soon be getting light, and we really may be seen unless we land our big fish first."

And without more ado he dragged the lifeless Levy ashore by the heels, while I alternately grasped the landing-stage to steady the boat, and did my best to protect the limp members and the leaden head from actual injury. All my efforts could not avert a few hard knocks, however, and these were sustained with such a horrifying insensibility of body and limb, that my worst suspicions were renewed before I crawled ashore myself, and remained kneeling over the prostrate form.

"Are you certain, Raffles?" I began, and could not finish the awful question.

"That he's alive?" said Raffles. "Rather, Bunny, and he'll be kicking below the belt again in a few more hours!"

"A few more *hours*, A.J.?"

"I give him four or five."

"Then it's concussion of the brain!"

"It's the brain all right," said Raffles. "But for 'concussion' I should say 'coma,' if I were you."

"What have I done!" I murmured, shaking my head over the poor old brute.

"You?" said Raffles. "Less than you think, perhaps!"

"But the man's never moved a muscle."

"Oh, yes, he has, Bunny!"

"When?"

"I'll tell you at the next stage," said Raffles. "Up with his heels and come this way."

And we trailed across a lawn so woefully neglected that the big body sagging between us, though it cleared the ground by several inches, swept the dew from the rank growth until we got it propped up on some steps at the base of the tower, and Raffles ran up to open the door. More steps there were within, stone steps allowing so little room for one foot and so much for the other as to suggest a spiral staircase from top to bottom of the tower. So it turned out to be; but there were landings communicating with the house, and on the first of them we laid our man and sat down to rest.

"How I love a silent, uncomplaining, stone staircase!" sighed the now quite invisible Raffles. "So of course we find one thrown away upon an empty house. Are you there, Bunny?"

"Rather! Are you quite sure nobody else is here?" I asked, for he was scarcely troubling to lower his voice.

"Only Levy, and he won't count till all hours."

"I'm waiting to hear how you know."

"Have a Sullivan, first."

"Are we as safe as all that?"

"If we're careful to make an ash-tray of our own pockets," said Raffles, and I heard him tapping his cigarette in the dark. I refused to run any risks. Next moment his match revealed him sitting at the bottom of one flight, and me at the top of the flight below; either spiral was lost in shadow; and all I saw besides was a cloud of smoke from the blood-stained lips of Raffles, more clouds of cobwebs, and Levy's boots lying over on their uppers, almost in my lap. Raffles called my attention to them before he blew out his match.

"He hasn't turned his toes up yet, you see! It's a hog's sleep, but not by any means his last."

"Did you mean just now that he woke up while I was in the boathouse?"

"Almost as soon as your back was turned, Bunny—if you call it waking up. You had knocked him out, you know, but only for a few minutes."

"Do you mean to tell me that he was none the worse?"

"Very little, Bunny."

My feeble heart jumped about in my body.

"Then what knocked him out again, A.J.?"

"I did."

"In the same way?"

"No, Bunny, he asked for a drink and I gave him one."

"A doctored drink!" I whispered with some horror; it was refreshing to feel once more horrified at some act not one's own.

"So to speak," said Raffles, with a gesture that I followed by the red end of his cigarette; "I certainly touched it up a bit, but I always meant to touch up his liquor if the beggar went back on his word. He did a good deal worse—for the second time of asking—and you did better than I ever knew you do before, Bunny! I simply carried on the good work. Our friend is full of a judicious blend of his own whiskey and the stuff poor Teddy had the other night. And when he does come to his senses I believe we shall find him damned sensible."

"And if he isn't, I suppose you'll keep him here until he is?"

"I shall hold him up to ransom," said Raffles, "at the top of this ruddy tower, until he pays through both nostrils for the privilege of climbing down alive."

"You mean until he stands by his side of your bargain?" said I, only hoping that was his meaning, but not without other apprehensions which Raffles speedily confirmed.

"And the rest!" he replied, significantly. "You don't suppose the skunk's going to get off as lightly as if he'd played the game, do you? I've got one of my own to play now, Bunny, and I mean to play it for all I'm worth. I thought it would come to this!"

In fact, he had foreseen treachery from the first, and the desperate device of kidnapping the traitor proved to have been as deliberate a move as Raffles had ever planned to meet a probable contingency. He had brought down a pair of handcuffs as well as a sufficient supply of Somnol. My own deed of violence was the one entirely unforeseen effect, and Raffles vowed it had been a help. But when I inquired whether he had ever been over this empty house before, an irritable jerk of his cigarette end foretold the answer.

"My good Bunny, is this a time for rotten questions? Of course I've been over the whole place; didn't I tell you I'd been spending the week-end in these parts? I got an order to view the place, and have bribed the gardener not to let anybody else see over it till I've made up my mind. The gardener's cottage is on the other side of the main road, which runs flush with the front of the house; there's a splendid garden on that side, but it takes him all his time to keep it up, so he's given up bothering about this bit here. He only sets foot in the house to show people over; his wife comes in sometimes to open the downstairs windows; the ones upstairs are never shut. So you perceive we shall be fairly free from interruption at the top of this tower, especially when I tell you that it finishes in a room as sound-proof as old Carlyle's crow's-nest in Cheyne Row."

It flashed across me that another great man of letters had made his local habitation if not his name in this part of the Thames Valley; and when I asked if this was that celebrity's house, Raffles seemed surprised that I had not recognised it as such in the dark. He said it would never let again, as the place was far too good for its position, which was now much too near London. He also told me that the idea of holding Dan Levy up to ransom had occurred to him when he found himself being followed about town by Levy's "mamelukes," and saw what a traitor he had to cope with.

"And I hope you like the idea, Bunny," he added, "because I was never caught kidnapping before, and in all London there wasn't a bigger man to kidnap."

"I love it," said I (and it was true enough of the abstract idea), "but don't you think he's just a bit too big? Won't the country ring with his disappearance?"

"My dear Bunny, nobody will dream he's disappeared!" said Raffles, confidently. "I know the habits of the beast; didn't I tell you he ran another show somewhere? Nobody seems to know where, but when he isn't here, that's where he's supposed to be, and when he's there he cuts town for days on end. I suppose you never noticed I've been wearing an overcoat all this time, Bunny?"

"Oh, yes, I did," said I. "Of course it's one of his?"

"The very one he'd have worn to-night, and his soft hat from the same peg is in one of the pockets; their absence won't look as if he'd come out feet first, will it, Bunny? I thought his stick might be in the way, so instead of bringing it too, I stowed it away behind his books. But these things will serve a second turn when we see our way to letting him go again like a gentleman."

The red end of the Sullivan went out sizzling between a moistened thumb and finger, and no doubt Raffles put it carefully in his pocket as he rose to resume the ascent. It was still perfectly dark on the tower stairs; but by the time we reached the sanctum at the top we could see each other's outlines against certain ovals of wild grey sky and dying stars. For there was a window more like a porthole in three of the four walls; in the fourth wall was a cavity like a ship's bunk, into which we lifted our still unconscious prisoner as gently as we might. Nor was that the last that was done for him, now that some slight amends were possible. From an invisible locker Raffles produced bundles of thin, coarse stuff, one of which he placed as a pillow under the sleeper's head, while the other was shaken out into a covering for his body.

"And you asked me if I'd ever been over the place!" said Raffles, putting a third bundle in my hands. "Why, I slept up here last night, just to see if it was all as quiet as it looked; these were my bed-clothes, and I want you to follow my example."

"I go to sleep?" I cried. "I couldn't and wouldn't for a thousand pounds, Raffles!"

"Oh, yes, you could!" said Raffles, and as he spoke there was a horrible explosion in the tower. Upon my word, I thought one of us was shot, until there came the smaller sounds of froth pattering on the floor and liquor bubbling from a bottle.

"Champagne!" I exclaimed, when he had handed me the metal cap of a flask, and I had taken a sip. "Did you hide that up here as well?"

"I hid nothing up here except myself," returned Raffles, laughing. "This is one of a couple of pints from the cellarette in Levy's billiard den; take your will of it, Bunny, and perhaps the old man may have the other when he's a good boy. I fancy we shall find it a stronger card than it looks. Meanwhile let sleeping dogs lie and lying dogs sleep! And you'd be far more use to me later, Bunny, if only you'd try to do the same."

I was beginning to feel that I might try, for Raffles was filling up the metal cup every minute, and also plying me with sandwiches from Levy's table, brought hence (with the champagne) in Levy's overcoat pocket. It was still pleasing to reflect that they had been originally intended for the rival bravos of Gray's Inn. But another idea that did occur to me, I dismissed at the time, and so justly that I would disabuse any other suspicious mind of it without delay. Dear old Raffles was scarcely more skilful and audacious as amateur cracksman than as amateur anaesthetist, nor was he ever averse from the practice of his uncanny genius at either game. But, sleepy as I soon found myself at the close of our very long night's work, I had no subsequent reason to suppose that Raffles had given *me* drop or morsel of anything but sandwiches and champagne.

So I rolled myself up on the locker, just as things were beginning to take visible shape even without the tower windows behind them, and I was almost dropping off to sleep when a sudden anxiety smote my mind.

"What about the boat?" I asked.

There was no answer.

"Raffles!" I cried. "What are you going to do about the beggar's boat?"

"You go to sleep," came the sharp reply, "and leave the boat to me."

And I fancied from his voice that Raffles also had lain him down, but on the floor.

XV

Trial by Raffles

When I awoke it was dazzling daylight in the tower, and the little scene was quite a surprise to me. It had felt far larger in the dark. I suppose the floor-space was about twelve feet square, but it was contracted on one side by the well and banisters of a wooden staircase from the room below, on another by the ship's bunk, and opposite that by the locker on which I lay. Moreover, the four walls, or rather the four triangles of roof, sloped so sharply to the apex of the tower as to leave an inner margin in which few grown persons could have stood upright. The port-hole windows were shrouded with rags of cobweb spotted with dead flies. They had evidently not been opened for years; it was even more depressingly obvious that we must not open them. One was thankful for such modicum of comparatively pure air as came up the open stair from the floor below; but in the freshness of the morning one trembled to anticipate the atmosphere of this stale and stuffy eyrie through the heat of a summer's day. And yet neither the size nor the scent of the place, nor any other merely scenic feature, was half so disturbing or fantastic as the appearance of my two companions.

Raffles, not quite at the top of the stairs, but near enough to loll over the banisters, and Levy, cumbering the ship's bunk, were indeed startling figures to an eye still dim with sleep. Raffles had an ugly cut from the left nostril to the corner of the mouth; he had washed the blood from his face, but the dark and angry streak remained to heighten his unusual pallor. Levy looked crumpled and debauched, flabbily and feebly senile, yet with his vital forces making a last flicker in his fiery eyes. He was grotesquely swathed in scarlet bunting, from which his doubled fists protruded in handcuffs; a bit of thin rope attached the handcuffs to a peg on which his coat and hat were also hanging, and a longer bit was taken round the banisters from the other end of the bunting, which I now perceived to be a tattered and torn Red Ensign. This led to the discovery that I myself had been sleeping in the Union Jack, and it brought my eyes back to the ghastly face of Raffles, who was already smiling at mine.

"Enjoyed your night under canvas, Bunny? Then you might get up and present your colours to the prisoner in the bunk. You needn't be frightened of him, Bunny; he's such a devilish tough customer that I've had to clap him in irons, as you see. Yet he can't say I haven't given him rope enough; he's got lashings of rope—eh, Bunny?"

"That's right!" said Levy, with a bitter snarl. "Get a man down by foul play, and then wipe your boots on him! I'd stick it like a lamb if only you'd give me that drink."

And then it was, as I got to my feet, and shook myself free from the folds of the Union Jack, that I saw the unopened pint of champagne standing against the banisters in full view of the bunk. I confess I eyed it wistfully myself; but Raffles was adamant alike to friend and foe, and merely beckoned me to follow him down the wooden stair, without answering Levy at all. I certainly thought it a risk to leave that worthy unwatched for a moment, but it was scarcely for more. The room below was fitted with a bath and a lavatory basin, which Raffles pointed out to me without going all the way down himself. At the same time he handed me a stale remnant of the sandwiches removed with Levy from his house.

"I'm afraid you'll have to wash these down at that tap," said he. "The poor devil has finished what you left at daybreak, besides making a hole in my flask; but he can't or won't eat a bite, and if only he stands his trial and takes his sentence like a man, I think he might have the other pint to his own infernal cheek."

"Trial and sentence!" I exclaimed. "I thought you were going to hold him up to ransom?"

"Not without a fair trial, my dear Bunny," said Raffles in the accents of reproof. "We must hear what the old swab has to say for himself, when he's heard what I've got to say to him. So you stick your head under the tap when you've had your snack, Bunny; it won't come up to the swim I had after I'd taken the boat back, when you and Shylock were fast asleep, but it's all you've time for if you want to hear me open my case."

And open it he did before himself, as judge and counsel in one, sitting on the locker as on the bench, the very moment I reappeared in court.

"Prisoner in the bunk, before we formulate the charge against you we had better deal with your last request for drink, made in the same breath as a preposterous complaint about foul play. The request has been made and granted more than once already this morning. This time it's refused. Drink has been your undoing, prisoner in the bunk; it is drink that necessitates your annual purification at Carlsbad, and yet within a week of that chastening experience you come before me without knowing where you are or how you got here."

"That wasn't the whisky," muttered Levy with a tortured brow. "That was something else, which you'll hear more about; foul play it was, and you'll pay for it yet. There's not a headache in a hogshead of my whisky."

"Well," resumed Raffles, "your champagne is on the same high level, and here's a pint of the best which you can open for yourself if only you show your sense before I've done with you. But you won't advance that little millennium by talking about foul play as though it were all on one side and the foulest of the foul not on yours. You will only retard the business of the court. You are indicted with extortion and sharp practice in all your dealings, with cheating and misleading your customers, attempting to cheat and betray your friends, and breaking all the rules of civilised crime. You are not invited to plead either way, because this court would not attach the slightest value to your plea; but presently you will get an opportunity of addressing the court in mitigation of your sentence. Or, if you like," continued Raffles, with a wink at me, "you may be represented by counsel. My learned friend here, I'm sure, will be proud to undertake your defence as a 'docker'; or—perhaps I should say a 'bunker,' Mr. Bunny?"

And Raffles laughed as coyly as a real judge at a real judicial joke, whereupon I joined in so uproariously as to find myself degraded from the position of leading counsel to that of the general public in a single flash from the judge's eye.

"If I hear any more laughter," said Raffles, "I shall clear the court. It's perfectly monstrous that people should come here to a court of justice and behave as though they were at a theatre."

Levy had been reclining with his yellow face twisted and his red eyes shut; but now these burst open as with flames, and the dry lips spat a hearty curse at the judge upon the locker.

"Take care!" said Raffles. "Contempt of court won't do you any good, you know!"

"And what good will all this foolery do you? Say what you've got to say against me, and be damned to you!"

"I fear you're confusing our functions sadly," said Raffles, with a compassionate shake of the head. "But so far as your first exhortation goes, I shall endeavour to take you at your word. You are a money-lender trading, among other places, in Jermyn Street, St. James's, under the style and title of Daniel Levy."

"It 'appens to be my name."

"That I can well believe," rejoined Raffles; "and if I may say so, Mr. Levy, I respect you for it. You don't call yourself MacGregor or Montgomery. You don't sail under false colours at all. You fly the skull and crossbones of Daniel Levy, and it's one of the points that distinguish you from the ruck of money-lenders and put you in a class by yourself. Unfortunately, the other points are not so creditable. If you are more brazen than most you are also more unscrupulous; if you fly at higher game, you descend to lower dodges. You may be the biggest man alive at your job; you are certainly the biggest villain."

"But I'm up against a bigger now," said Levy, shifting his position and closing his crimson eyes.

"Possibly," said Raffles, as he produced a long envelope and unfolded a sheet of foolscap; "but permit me to remind you of a few of your own proven villainies before you take any more shots at mine. Last year you had three of your great bargains set aside by the law as hard and unconscionable; but every year you have these cases, and at best the terms are modified in favour of your wretched client. But it's only the exception who will face the music of the law-courts and the Press, and you figure on the general run. You prefer people like the Lincolnshire vicar you hounded into an asylum the year before last. You cherish the memory of the seven poor devils that you drove to suicide between 1890 and 1894; that sort pay the uttermost farthing before the debt to nature! You set great store by the impoverished gentry and nobility who have you to stay with them when the worst comes to the worst, and secure a respite in exchange for introductions to their pals. No fish is too large for your net, and none is too small, from his highness of Hathipur to that poor little builder at Bromley, who cut the throats—"

"Stop it!" cried Levy, in a lather of impotent rage.

"By all means," said Raffles, restoring the paper to its envelope. "It's an ugly little load for one man's soul, I admit; but you must see it was about time somebody beat you at your own beastly game."

"It's a pack of blithering lies," retorted Levy, "and you haven't beaten me yet. Stick to facts within your own knowledge, and then tell me if your precious Garlands haven't brought their troubles on themselves?"

"Certainly they have," said Raffles. "But it isn't your treatment of the Garlands that has brought you to this pretty pass."

"What is it, then?"

"Your treatment of me, Mr. Levy."

E.W. HORNUNG

"A cursed crook like you!"

"A party to a pretty definite bargain, however, and a discredited person only so far as that bargain is concerned."

"And the rest!" said the money-lender, jeering feebly. "I know more about you than you guess."

"I should have put it the other way round," replied Raffles, smiling. "But we are both forgetting ourselves, prisoner in the bunk. Kindly note that your trial is resumed, and further contempt will not be allowed to go unpurged. You referred a moment ago to my unfortunate friends; you say they were the engineers of their own misfortunes. That might be said of all who ever put themselves in your clutches. You squeeze them as hard as the law will let you, and in this case I don't see how the law is to interfere. So I interfere myself—in the first instance as disastrously as you please."

"You did so!" exclaimed Levy, with a flicker of his inflamed eyes. "You brought things to a head; that's all *you* did."

"On the contrary, you and I came to an agreement which still holds good," said Raffles, significantly. "You are to return me a certain note of hand for thirteen thousand and odd pounds, taken in exchange for a loan of ten thousand, and you are also to give an understanding to leave another fifteen thousand of yours on mortgage for another year at least, instead of foreclosing, as you threatened and had a right to do this week. That was your side of the bargain."

"Well," said Levy, "and when did I go back on it?"

"My side," continued Raffles, ignoring the interpolation, "was to get you by hook or crook a certain letter which you say you never wrote. As a matter of fact it was only to be got by crook—"

"Aha!"

"I got hold of it, nevertheless. I brought it to you at your house last night. And you instantly destroyed it after as foul an attack as one man ever made upon another!"

Raffles had risen in his wrath, was towering over the prostrate prisoner, forgetful of the mock trial, dead even to the humour which he himself had infused into a sufficiently lurid situation, but quite terribly alive to the act of treachery and violence which had brought that situation about. And I must say that Levy looked no less alive to his own enormity; he quailed in his bonds with a guilty fearfulness strange to witness in so truculent a brute; and it was with something near a quaver that his voice came next.

"I know that was wrong," the poor devil owned. "I'm very sorry for it, I'm sure! But you wouldn't trust me with my own property, and that and the drink together made me mad."

"So you acknowledge the alcoholic influence at last?"

"Oh, yes! I must have been as drunk as an owl."

"You know you've been suggesting that we drugged you?"

"Not seriously, Mr. Raffles. I knew the old stale taste too well. It must have been the best part of a bottle I had before you got down."

"In your anxiety to see me safe and sound?"

"That's it—with the letter."

"You never dreamt of playing me false until I hesitated to let you handle it?"

"Never for one moment, my dear Raffles!"

Raffles was still standing up to his last inch under the apex of the tower, his head and shoulders the butt of a climbing sunbeam full of fretful motes. I could not see his expression from the banisters, but only its effect upon Dan Levy, who first held up his manacled hands in hypocritical protestation, and then dropped them as though it were a bad job.

"Then why," said Raffles, "did you have me watched almost from the moment that we parted company at the Albany last Friday morning?"

"*I* have you watched!" exclaimed the other in real horror. "Why should I? It must have been the police."

"It was not the police, though the blackguards did their best to look as if they were. I happen to be too familiar with both classes to be deceived. Your fellows were waiting for me up at Lord's, but I had no difficulty in shaking them off when I got back to the Albany. They gave me no further trouble until last night, when they got on my tracks at Gray's Inn in the guise of the two common, low detectives whom I believe I have already mentioned to you."

"You said you left them there in their glory."

"It was glorious from my point of view rather than theirs."

Levy struggled into a less recumbent posture.

"And what makes you think," said he, "that I set this watch upon you?"

"I don't think," returned Raffles. "I know."

"And how the devil do you know?"

Raffles answered with a slow smile, and a still slower shake of the head: "You really mustn't ask me to give everybody away, Mr. Levy!"

The money-lender swore an oath of sheer incredulous surprise, but checked himself at that and tried one more poser.

"And what do you suppose was my object in having you watched, if it wasn't to ensure your safety?"

"It might have been to make doubly sure of the letter, and to cut down expenses at the same swoop, by knocking me on the head and abstracting the treasure from my person. It was a jolly cunning idea—prisoner in the bunk! I shouldn't be upset about it just because it didn't come off. My compliments especially on making up your varlets in the quite colourable image of the true detective. If they had fallen upon me, and it had been a case of my liberty or your letter, you know well enough which I should let go."

But Levy had fallen back upon his pillow of folded flag, and the Red Ensign over him bubbled and heaved with his impotent paroxysms.

"They told you! They must have told you!" he ground out through his teeth. "The traitors—the blasted traitors!"

"It's a catching complaint, you see, Mr. Levy," said Raffles, "especially when one's elders and betters themselves succumb to it."

"But they're such liars!" cried Levy, shifting his ground again. "Don't you see what liars they are? I did set them to watch you, but for your own good, as I've just been telling you. I was so afraid something might 'appen to you; they were there to see that nothing did. Now do you spot their game? I'd got to take the skunks into the secret, more or less, an' they've played it double on us both. Meant bagging the letter from you to blackmail me with it; that's what they meant! Of course, when they failed to bring it off, they'd pitch any yarn to you. But that was their game all right. You must see for yourself it could never have been mine, Raffles, and—and let me out o' this, like a good feller!"

"Is this your defence?" asked Raffles as he resumed his seat on the judicial locker.

"Isn't it your own?" the other asked in his turn, with an eager removal of all resentment from his manner. "'Aven't we both been got at by those two jackets? Of course I was sorry ever to 'ave trusted 'em an inch, and you were quite right to serve me as you did if what they'd been telling you 'ad been the truth; but, now you see it was all a pack of lies it's surely about time to stop treating me like a mad dog."

"Then you really mean to stand by your side of the original arrangement?"

"Always did," declared our captive; "never 'ad the slightest intention of doing anything else."

"Then where's the first thing you promised me in fair exchange for what you destroyed last night? Where's Mr. Garland's note of hand?"

"In my pocket-book, and that's in my pocket."

"In case the worst comes to the worst," murmured Raffles in sly commentary, and with a sidelong glance at me.

"What's that? Don't you believe me? I'll 'and it over this minute, if only you'll take these damned things off my wrists. There's no excuse for 'em now, you know!"

Raffles shook his head.

"I'd rather not trust myself within reach of your raw fists yet, prisoner. But my marshal will produce the note from your person if it's there."

It was there, in a swollen pocket-book which I replaced otherwise intact while Raffles compared the signature on the note of hand with samples which he had brought with him for the purpose.

"It's genuine enough," said Levy, with a sudden snarl and a lethal look that I intercepted at close quarters.

"So I perceive," said Raffles. "And now I require an equally genuine signature to this little document which is also a part of your bond."

The little document turned out to be a veritable Deed, engrossed on parchment, embossed with a ten-shilling stamp, and duly calling itself an INDENTURE, in fourteenth century capitals. So much I saw as I held it up for the prisoner to read over. The illegally legal instrument is still in existence, with its unpunctuated jargon about "hereditaments" and "fee simple," its "and whereas the said Daniel Levy" in every other line, and its eventual plain provision for "the said sum of £15,000 to remain charged upon the security of the hereditaments in the said recited Indenture. . . until the expiration of one year computed from—" that summer's day in that empty tower! The whole thing had been properly and innocently prepared by old Mother Hubbard, the "little solicitor" whom Raffles had mentioned as having been in our house at school, from a copy of the original mortgage deed supplied in equal innocence by Mr. Garland. I sometimes wonder what those worthy citizens would have said, if they had dreamt for a moment under what conditions of acute duress their deed was to be signed!

Signed it was, however, and with less demur than might have been expected of so inveterate a fighter as Dan Levy. But his one remaining course was obviously the line of least resistance; no other would square with his ingenious repudiation of the charge of treachery to Raffles, much less with his repeated protestations that he had always intended to perform his part of their agreement. It was to his immediate interest to convince us of his good faith, and up to this point he might well have thought he had succeeded in so doing. Raffles had concealed his full knowledge of the creature's duplicity, had enjoyed leading him on from lie to lie, and I had enjoyed listening almost as much as I now delighted in the dilemma in which Levy had landed himself; for either he must sign and look pleasant, or else abandon his innocent posture altogether; and so he looked as pleasant as he could, and signed in his handcuffs, with but the shadow of a fight for their immediate removal.

"And now," said Levy, when I had duly witnessed his signature, "I think I've about earned that little drop of my own champagne."

"Not quite yet," replied Raffles, in a tone like thin ice. "We are only at the point we should have reached the moment I arrived at your house last night; you have now done under compulsion what you had agreed to do of your own free will then."

Levy lay back in the bunk, plunged in billows of incongruous bunting, with fallen jaw and fiery eyes, an equal blend of anger and alarm. "But I told you I wasn't myself last night," he whined. "I've said I was very sorry for all I done, but can't 'ardly remember doing. I say it again from the bottom of my 'eart."

"I've no doubt you do," said Raffles. "But what you did after our arrival was nothing to what you had already done; it was only the last of those acts of treachery for which you are still on your trial—prisoner in the bunk!"

"But I thought I'd explained all the rest?" cried the prisoner, in a palsy of impotent rage and disappointment.

"You have," said Raffles, "in the sense of making your perfidy even plainer than it was before. Come, Mr. Levy! I know every move you've made, and the game's been up longer than you think; you won't score a point by telling lies that contradict each other and aggravate your guilt. Have you nothing better to say why the sentence of the court should not be passed upon you?"

A sullen silence was broken by a more precise and staccato repetition of the question. And then to my amazement, I beheld the gross lower lip of Levy actually trembling, and a distressing flicker of the inflamed eyelids.

"I felt you'd swindled me," he quavered out "And I thought—I'd swindle—you."

"Bravo!" cried Raffles. "That's the first honest thing you've said; let me tell you, for your encouragement, that it reduces your punishment by twenty-five per cent. You will, nevertheless, pay a fine of fifteen hundred pounds for your latest little effort in low treason."

Though not unprepared for some such ultimatum, I must own I heard it with dismay. On all sorts of grounds, some of them as unworthy as itself, this last demand failed to meet with my approval; and I determined to expostulate with Raffles before it was too late. Meanwhile I hid my feelings as best I could, and admired the spirit with which Dan Levy expressed his.

"I'll see you damned first!" he cried. "It's blackmail!"

"Guineas," said Raffles, "for contempt of court."

And more to my surprise than ever, not a little indeed to my secret disappointment, our captive speedily collapsed again, whimpering, moaning, gnashing his teeth, and clutching at the Red Ensign, with closed eyes and distorted face, so much as though he were about to have a fit that I caught up the half-bottle of champagne, and began removing the wire at a nod from Raffles.

"Don't cut the string just yet," he added, however, with an eye on Levy—who instantly opened his.

"I'll pay up!" he whispered, feebly yet eagerly. "It serves me right. I promise I'll pay up!"

"Good!" said Raffles. "Here's your own cheque-book from your own room, and here's my fountain pen."

"You won't take my word?"

"It's quite enough to have to take your cheque; it should have been hard cash."

"So it shall be, Raffles, if you come up with me to my office!"

"I dare say."

"To my bank, then!"

"I prefer to go alone. You will kindly make it an open cheque payable to bearer."

The fountain pen was poised over the chequebook, but only because I had placed it in Levy's fingers, and was holding the cheque-book under them.

"And what if I refuse?" he demanded, with a last flash of his native spirit.

"We shall say good-bye, and give you until to-night."

"All day to call for help in!" muttered Levy, all but to himself.

"Do you happen to know where you are?" Raffles asked him.

"No, but I can find out."

"If you knew already you would also know that you might call till you were black in the face; but to keep you in blissful ignorance you will be bound a good deal more securely than you are at present. And to spare your poor voice you will also be very thoroughly gagged."

Levy took remarkably little notice of either threat or gibe.

"And if I give in and sign?" said he, after a pause.

"You will remain exactly as you are, with one of us to keep you company, while the other goes up to town to cash your cheque. You can't expect me to give you a chance of stopping it, you know."

This, again, struck me as a hard condition, if only prudent when one came to think of it from our point of view; still, it took even me by surprise, and I expected Levy to fling away the pen in disgust. He balanced it, however, as though also weighing the two alternatives very carefully in his mind, and during his deliberations his bloodshot eyes wandered from Raffles to me and back again to Raffles. In a word, the latest prospect appeared to disturb Mr. Levy less than, for obvious reasons, it did me. Certainly for him it was the lesser of the two evils, and as such he seemed to accept it when he finally wrote out the cheque for fifteen hundred guineas (Raffles insisting on these), and signed it firmly before sinking back as though exhausted by the effort.

Raffles was as good as his word about the champagne now: dram by dram he poured the whole pint into the cup belonging to his flask, and dram by dram our prisoner tossed it off, but with closed eyes, like a delirious invalid, and towards the end, with a head so heavy that Raffles had to raise it from the rolled flag, though foul talons still came twitching out for more. It was an unlovely process, I will confess; but what was a pint, as Raffles said? At any rate I could bear him out that these potations had not been hocussed, and Raffles whispered the same for the flask which he handed me with Levy's revolver at the head of the wooden stairs.

"I'm coming down," said I, "for a word with you in the room below."

Raffles looked at me with open eyes, then more narrowly at the red lids of Levy, and finally at his own watch.

"Very well, Bunny, but I must cut and run for my train in about a minute. There's a 9.24 which would get me to the bank before eleven, and back here by one or two."

"Why go to the bank at all?" I asked him point-blank in the lower room.

"To cash his cheque before he has a chance of stopping it. Would you like to go instead of me, Bunny?"

"No, thank you!"

"Well, don't get hot about it; you've got the better billet of the two."

"The softer one, perhaps."

"Infinitely, Bunny, with the old bird full of his own champagne, and his own revolver in your pocket or your hand! The worst he can do is to start yelling out, and I really do believe that not a soul would hear him if he did. The gardeners are always at work on the other side of the main road. A passing boatload is the only danger, and I doubt if even they would hear."

"My billet's all right," said I, valiantly. "It's yours that worries me."

"Mine!" cried Raffles, with an almost merry laugh. "My dear, good Bunny, you may make your mind easy about my little bit! Of course, it'll take some doing at the bank. I don't say it's a straight part there. But trust me to play it on my head."

"Raffles," I said, in a low voice that may have trembled, "it's not a part for you to play at all! I don't mean the little bit at the bank. I mean this whole blackmailing part of the business. It's not like you, Raffles. It spoils the whole thing!"

I had got it off my chest without a hitch. But so far Raffles had not discouraged me. There was a look on his face which even made me think that he agreed with me in his heart. Both hardened as he thought it over.

"It's Levy who's spoilt the whole thing," he rejoined obdurately in the end. "He's been playing me false all the time, and he's got to pay for it."

"But you never meant to make anything out of him, A.J.!"

"Well, I do now, and I've told you why. Why shouldn't I?"

"Because it's not your game!" I cried, with all the eager persuasion in my power. "Because it's the sort of thing Dan Levy would do himself—it's *his* game, all right—it simply drags you down to his level—"

But there he stopped me with a look, and not the kind of look I often had from Raffles, It was no new feat of mine to make him angry, scornful, bitterly cynical or sarcastic. This, however, was a look of pain and even shame, as though he had suddenly seen himself in a new and peculiarly unlovely light.

E.W. HORNUNG

"Down to it!" he exclaimed, with an irony that was not for me. "As though there could be a much lower level than mine! Do you know, Bunny, I sometimes think my moral sense is ahead of yours?"

I could have laughed outright; but the humour that was the salt of him seemed suddenly to have gone out of Raffles.

"I know what I am," said he, "but I'm afraid you're getting a hopeless villain-worshipper!"

"It's not the villain I care about," I answered, meaning every word. "It's the sportsman behind the villain, as you know perfectly well."

"I know the villain behind the sportsman rather better," replied Raffles, laughing when I least expected it. "But you're by way of forgetting his existence altogether. I shouldn't wonder if some day you wrote me up into a heavy hero, Bunny, and made me turn in my quicklime! Let this remind you what I always was and shall be to the end."

And he took my hand, as I fondly hoped in surrender to my appeal to those better feelings which I knew I had for once succeeded in quickening within him.

But it was only to bid me a mischievous goodbye, ere he ran down the spiral stair, leaving me to listen till I lost his feathery foot-falls in the base of the tower, and then to mount guard over my tethered, handcuffed, somnolent, and yet always formidable prisoner at the top.

XVI

Watch and Ward

I well remember, as I set reluctant foot upon the wooden stair, taking a last and somewhat lingering look at the dust and dirt of the lower chamber, as one who knew not what might happen before he saw it again. The stain as of red rust in the lavatory basin, the gritty deposit in the bath, the verdigris on all the taps, the foul opacity of the windows, are among the trivialities that somehow stamped themselves upon my mind. One of the windows was open at the top, had been so long open that the aperture was curtained with cobwebs at each extremity, but in between I got quite a poignant picture of the Thames as I went upstairs. It was only a sinuous perspective of sunlit ripples twinkling between wooded gardens and open meadows, a fisherman or two upon the tow-path, a canoe in mid-stream, a gaunt church crowning all against the sky. But inset in such surroundings it was like a flash from a magic-lantern in a coal-cellar. And very loth was I to exchange that sunny peep for an indefinite prospect of my prisoner's person at close quarters.

Yet the first stage of my vigil proved such a sinecure as to give me some confidence for all the rest. Dan Levy opened neither his lips nor his eyes at my approach, but lay on his back with the Red Ensign drawn up to his chin, and the peaceful countenance of profound oblivion. I remember taking a good look at him, and thinking that his face improved remarkably in repose, that in death he might look fine. The forehead was higher and broader than I had realised, the thick lips were firm enough now, but the closing of the crafty little eyes was the greatest gain of all. On the whole, not only a better but a stronger face than it had been all the morning, a more formidable face by far. But the man had fallen asleep in his bonds, and forgotten them; he would wake up abject enough; if not, I had the means to reduce him to docility. Meanwhile, I was in no hurry to show my power, but stole on tiptoe to the locker, and took my seat by inches.

Levy did not move a muscle. No sound escaped him either, and somehow or other I should have expected him to snore; indeed, it might have come as a relief, for the silence of the tower soon got upon my nerves. It was not a complete silence; that was (and always is) the worst of it. The wooden stairs creaked more than once; there were little rattlings, faint and distant, as of a dried leaf or a loose window, in the bowels of the house; and though nothing came of any of these noises, except a fresh period of tension on my part, they made the skin act on my forehead every time. Then I remember a real anxiety over a blue-bottle, that must have come in through the open window just below, for suddenly it buzzed into my ken and looked like attacking Levy on the spot. Somehow I slew it with less noise than the brute itself was making; and not until after that breathless achievement did I realise how anxious I was to keep my prisoner asleep. Yet I had the revolver, and he lay handcuffed and bound down! It was in the next long silence that I became sensitive to another sound which indeed I had heard at intervals already, only to dismiss it from my mind as one of the signs of extraneous life which were bound to penetrate even to the top of my tower. It was a slow and regular beat, as of a sledge-hammer in a distant forge, or some sort of machinery only audible when there was absolutely nothing else to be heard. It could hardly be near at hand, for I could not hear it properly unless I held my breath. Then, however, it was always there, a sound that never ceased or altered, so that in the end I sat and listened to it and nothing else. I was not even looking at Levy when he asked me if I knew what it was.

His voice was quiet and civil enough, but it undoubtedly made me jump, and that brought a malicious twinkle into the little eyes that looked as though they had been studying me at their leisure. They were perhaps less violently bloodshot than before, the massive features calm and strong as they had been in slumber or its artful counterfeit.

"I thought you were asleep?" I snapped, and knew better for certain before he spoke.

"You see, that pint o' pop did me prouder than intended," he explained. "It's made a new man o' me, you'll be sorry to 'ear."

I should have been sorrier to believe it, but I did not say so, or anything else just then. The dull and distant beat came back to the ear. And Levy again inquired if I knew what it was.

"Do you?" I demanded.

"Rather!" he replied, with cheerful certitude. "It's the clock, of course."

"What clock?"

"The one on the tower, a bit lower down, facing the road."

"How do *you* know?" I demanded, with uneasy credulity.

"My good young man," said Dan Levy, "I know the face of that clock as well as I know the inside of this tower."

"Then you do know where you are!" I cried, in such surprise that Levy grinned in a way that ill became a captive.

"Why," said he, "I sold the last tenant up, and nearly took the 'ouse myself instead o' the place I got. It was what first attracted me to the neighbour'ood."

"Why couldn't you tell us the truth before?" I demanded, but my warmth merely broadened his grin.

"Why should I? It sometimes pays to seem more at a loss than you are."

"It won't in this case," said I through my teeth. But for all my austerity, and all his bonds, the prisoner continued to regard me with quiet but most disquieting amusement.

"I'm not so sure of that," he observed at length. "It rather paid, to my way of thinking, when Raffles went off to cash my cheque, and left you to keep an eye on me."

"Oh, did it!" said I, with pregnant emphasis, and my right hand found comfort in my jacket pocket, on the butt of the old brute's own weapon.

"I only mean," he rejoined, in a more conciliatory voice, "that you strike me as being more open to reason than your flash friend."

I said nothing to that.

"On the other 'and," continued Levy, still more deliberately, as though he really was comparing us in his mind; "on the other *hand*" stooping to pick up what he had dropped, "you don't take so many risks. Raffles takes so many that he's bound to land you both in the jug some day, if he hasn't done it this time. I believe he has, myself. But it's no use hollering before you're out o' the wood."

I agreed, with more confidence than I felt.

"Yet I wonder he never thought of it," my prisoner went on as if to himself.

"Thought of what?"

"Only the clock. He must've seen it before, if you never did; you don't tell me this little bit o' kidnapping was a sudden idea! It's all been thought out and the ground gone over, and the clock seen, as I say. Seen going. Yet it never strikes our flash friend that a going clock's got to be wound up once a week, and it might be as well to find out which day!"

"How do you know he didn't?"

"Because this 'appens to be the day!"

And Levy lay back in the bunk with the internal chuckle that I was beginning to know so well, but had little thought to hear from him in his present predicament. It galled me the more because I felt that Raffles would certainly not have heard it in my place. But at least I had the satisfaction of flatly and profanely refusing to believe the prisoner's statement.

"That be blowed for a bluff!" was more or less what I said. "It's too much of a coincidence to be anything else."

"The odds are only six to one against it," said Levy, indifferently. "One of you takes them with his eyes open. It seems rather a pity that the other should feel bound to follow him to certain ruin. But I suppose you know your own business best."

"At all events," I boasted, "I know better than to be bluffed by the most obvious lie I ever heard in my life. You tell me how you know about the man coming to wind the clock, and I may listen to you."

"I know because I know the man; little Scotchman he is, nothing to run away from—though he looks as hard as nails—what there is of him," said Levy, in a circumstantial and impartial flow that could not but carry some conviction. "He comes over from Kingston every Tuesday on his bike; some time before lunch he comes, and sees to my own clocks on the same trip. That's how I know. But you needn't believe me if you don't like."

"And where exactly does he come to wind this clock? I see nothing that can possibly have to do with it up here."

"No," said Levy; "he comes no higher than the floor below." I seemed to remember a kind of cupboard at the head of the spiral stair. "But that's near enough."

"You mean that we shall hear him?"

"And he us!" added Levy, with unmistakable determination.

"Look here, Mr. Levy," said I, showing him his own revolver, "if we do hear anybody, I shall hold this to your head, and if he does hear us I shall blow out your beastly brains!"

The mere feeling that I was, perhaps, the last person capable of any such deed enabled me to grind out this shocking threat in a voice worthy of it, and with a face, I hoped, not less in keeping. It was all the more mortifying when Dan Levy treated my tragedy as farce; in fact, if anything could have made me as bad as my word, it would have been the guttural laugh with which he greeted it.

"Excuse me," said he, dabbing his red eyes with the edge of the red bunting, "but the thought of your letting that thing off in order to preserve silence—why, it's as droll as your whole attempt to play the cold-blooded villain—*you*!"

"I shall play him to some purpose," I hissed, "if you drive me to it. I laid you out last night, remember, and for two pins I'll do the same thing again this morning. So now you know."

"That wasn't in cold blood," said Levy, rolling his head from side to side; "that was when the lot of us were brawling in our cups. I don't count that. You're in a false position, my dear sir. I don't mean last night or this morning—though I can see that you're no brigand or blackmailer at bottom—and I shouldn't wonder if you never forgave Raffles for letting you in for this partic'lar part of this partic'lar job. But that isn't what I mean. You've got in with a villain, but you ain't one yourself; that's where you're in the false position. He's the magsman, you're only the swell. *I* can see that. But the judge won't. You'll both get served the same, and in your case it'll be a thousand shames!"

He had propped himself on one elbow, and was speaking eagerly, persuasively, with almost a fatherly solicitude; yet I felt that both his words and their effect on me were being weighed and measured with meticulous discretion. And I encouraged him with a countenance as deliberately rueful and depressed, to an end which had only occurred to me with the significance of his altered tone.

"I can't help it," I muttered. "I must go through with the whole thing now."

"Why must you?" demanded Levy. "You've been led into a job that's none of your business, on be'alf of folks who're no friends of yours, and the job's developed into a serious crime, and the crime's going to be found out before you're an hour older. Why go through with it to certain quod?"

"There's nothing else for it," I answered, with a sulky resignation, though my pulse was quick with eagerness for what I felt was coming.

And then it came.

"Why not get out of the whole thing," suggested Levy, boldly, "before it's too late?"

"How can I?" said I, to lead him on with a more explicit proposition.

"By first releasing me, and then clearing out yourself!"

I looked at him as though this was certainly an idea, as though I were actually considering it in spite of myself and Raffles; and his eagerness fed upon my apparent indecision. He held up his fettered hands, begging and cajoling me to remove his handcuffs, and I, instead of telling him it was not in my power to do so until Raffles returned, pretended to hesitate on quite different grounds.

"It's all very well," I said, "but are you going to make it worth my while?"

"Certainly!" cried he. "Give me my chequebook out of my own pocket, where you were good enough to stow it before that blackguard left, and I'll write you one cheque for a hundred now, and another for another hundred before I leave this tower."

"You really will?" I temporised.

"I swear it!" he asseverated; and I still believe he might have kept his word about that. But now I knew where he *had* been lying to me, and now was the time to let him know I knew it.

"Two hundred pounds," said I, "for the liberty you are bound to get for nothing, as you yourself have pointed out, when the man turns up to wind the clock? A couple of hundred to save less than a couple of hours?"

Levy changed colour as he saw his mistake, and his eyes flashed with sudden fury; otherwise his self-command was only less admirable than his presence of mind.

"It wasn't to save time," said he; "it was to save my face in the neighbourhood. The well-known money-lender found bound and handcuffed in an empty house! It means the first laugh at my expense, whoever has the last laugh. But you're quite right; it wasn't worth two hundred golden sovereigns. Let them laugh! At any rate you and your flash friend'll be laughing on the wrong side of your mouths before the day's out. So that's all there is to it, and you'd better start screwing up your courage if you want to do me in! I did mean to give you another chance in life—but by God I wouldn't now if you were to go down on your knees for one!"

Considering that he was bound and I was free, that I was armed and he defenceless, there was perhaps more humour than the prisoner saw in his picture of me upon my knees to him. Not that I saw it all at once myself. I was too busy wondering whether there could be anything in his clock-winding story after all. Certainly it was inconsistent with the big bribe offered for his immediate freedom; but it was with something more than mere adroitness that the money-lender had reconciled the two things. In his place I should have been no less anxious to keep my humiliating experience a secret from the world; with his means I could conceive myself prepared to pay as dearly for such secrecy. On the other hand, if his idea was to stop the huge cheque already given to Raffles, then there was indeed no time to be lost, and the only wonder was that Levy should have waited so long before making overtures to me.

Raffles had now been gone a very long time, as it seemed to me, but my watch had run down, and the clock on the tower did not strike. Why they kept it going at all was a mystery to me; but now that Dan Levy was lying still again, with set teeth and inexorable eyes, I heard it beating out the seconds more than ever like a distant sledgehammer, and sixty of these I counted up into a minute of such portentous duration that what had seemed many hours to me might easily have been less than one. I only knew that the sun, which had begun by pouring in at one port-hole and out at the other, which had bathed the prisoner in his bunk about the time of his trial by Raffles, now crowned me with fire if I sat upon the locker, and made its varnish sticky if I did not. The atmosphere of the place was fast becoming unendurable in its unwholesome heat and sour stagnation. I sat in my shirt-sleeves at the top of the stairs, where one got such air as entered by the open window below. Levy had kicked off his covering of scarlet bunting, with a sudden oath which must have been the only sound within the tower for an hour at least; all the rest of the time he lay with fettered fists clenched upon his breast, with fierce eyes fixed upon the top of the bunk, and something about the whole man that I was forced to watch, something indomitable and intensely alert, a curious suggestion of smouldering fires on the point of leaping into flame.

I feared this man in my heart of hearts. I may as well admit it frankly. It was not that he was twice my size, for I had the like advantage in point of years; it was not that I had any reason to distrust the strength of his bonds or the efficacy of the weapon in my possession. It was a question of personality, not of material advantage or disadvantage, or of physical fear at all. It was simply the spirit of the man that dominated mine. I felt that my mere flesh and blood would at any moment give a good account of his, as well they might with the odds that were on my side. Yet that did not lessen the sense of subtle and essential inferiority, which grew upon my nerves with almost every minute of that endless morning, and made me long for the relief of physical contest even on equal terms. I could have set the old ruffian free, and thrown his revolver out of the window, and then said to him, "Come on! Your weight against my age, and may the devil take the worse man!" Instead, I must sit glaring at him to mask my qualms. And after much thinking about the kind of conflict that could never be, in the end came one of a less heroic but not less desperate type, before there was time to think at all.

Levy had raised his head, ever so little, but yet enough for my vigilance. I saw him listening. I listened too. And down below in the core of the tower I heard, or thought I heard, a step like a feather, and then after some moments another. But I had spent those moments in gazing instinctively down the stair; it was the least rattle of the handcuffs that brought my eyes like lightning back to the bunk; and there was Levy with hollow palms about his mouth, and his mouth wide open for the roar that my own palms stifled in his throat.

Indeed, I had leapt upon him once more like a fiend, and for an instant I enjoyed a shameful advantage; it can hardly have lasted longer. The brute first bit me through the hand, so that I carry his mark to this day; then, with his own hands, he took me by the throat, and I thought that my last moments were come. He squeezed so hard that I thought my windpipe must burst, thought my eyes must leave their sockets. It was the grip of a gorilla, and it was accompanied by a spate of curses and the grin of a devil incarnate. All my dreams of equal combat had not prepared me for superhuman power on his part, such utter impotence on mine. I tried to wrench myself from his murderous clasp, and was nearly felled by the top of the bunk. I hurled myself out sideways, and out he came after me, tearing down the peg to which his handcuffs were tethered; that only gave him the better grip upon my throat, and he never relaxed it for an instant, scrambling to his feet when I staggered to mine, for by them alone was he fast now to the banisters.

Meanwhile I was feeling in an empty pocket for his revolver, which had fallen out as we struggled on the floor. I saw it there now with my starting eyeballs, kicked about by our shuffling feet. I tried to make a dive for it, but Levy had seen it also, and he kicked it through the banisters without relaxing his murderous hold. I could have sworn afterwards that I heard the weapon fall with a clatter on the wooden stairs. But what I still remember hearing most distinctly (and feeling hot upon my face) is the stertorous breathing that was unbroken by a single syllable after the first few seconds.

It was a brutal encounter, not short and sharp like the one overnight, but horribly protracted. Nor was all the brutality by any means on one side; neither will I pretend that I was getting much more than my deserts in the defeat that threatened to end in my extinction. Not for an instant had my enemy loosened his deadly clutch, and now he had me penned against the banisters, and my one hope was that they would give way before our united weight, and precipitate us both into the room below. That would be better than being slowly throttled, even if it were only a better death. Other chance there was none, and I was actually trying to fling myself over, beating the air with both hands wildly, when one of them closed upon the butt of the revolver that I thought had been kicked into the room below!

I was too far gone to realise that a miracle had happened—to be so much as puzzled by it then. But I was not too far gone to use that revolver, and to use it as I would have done on cool reflection. I thrust it under my opponent's armpit, and I fired through into space. The report was deafening. It did its work. Levy let go of me, and staggered back as though I had really shot him. And that instant I was brandishing his weapon in his face.

"You tried to shoot me! You tried to shoot me!" he gasped twice over through a livid mask.

"No, I didn't!" I panted. "I tried to frighten you, and I jolly well succeeded! But I'll shoot you like a dog if you don't get back to your kennel and lie down."

He sat and gasped upon the side of the bunk. There was no more fight in him. His very lips were blue. I put the pistol back in my pocket, and retracted my threat in a sudden panic.

"There! It's your own fault if you so much as see it again," I promised him, in a breathless disorder only second to his own.

"But you jolly nearly strangled me. And now we're a pretty pair!"

His hands grasped the edge of the bunk, and he leant his weight on them, breathing very hard. It might have been an attack of asthma, or it might have been a more serious seizure, but it was a case for stimulants if ever I saw one, and in the nick of time I remembered the flask that Raffles had left with me. It was the work of a very few seconds to pour out a goodly ration, and of but another for Daniel Levy to toss off the raw spirit like water. He was begging for more before I had helped myself. And more I gave him in the end; for it was no small relief to me to watch the leaden hue disappearing from the flabby face, and the laboured breathing gradually subside, even if it meant a renewal of our desperate hostilities.

But all that was at an end; the man was shaken to the core by his perfectly legitimate attempt at my destruction. He looked dreadfully old and hideous as he got bodily back into the bunk of his own accord. There, when I had yielded to his further importunities, and the flask was empty, he fell at length into a sleep as genuine as the last was not; and I was still watching over the poor devil, keeping the flies off him, and sometimes fanning him with a flag, less perhaps from humane motives than to keep him quiet as long as possible, when Raffles returned to light up the tableau like a sinister sunbeam.

Raffles had had his own adventures in town, and I soon had reason to feel thankful that I had not gone up instead of him. It seemed he had foreseen from the first the possibility of trouble at the bank over a large and absolutely open cheque. So he had gone first to the Chelsea studio in which he played the painter who never painted but kept a whole wardrobe of disguises for the models he never hired. Thence he had issued on this occasion in the living image of a well-known military man about town who was also well known to be a client of Dan Levy's. Raffles said the cashier stared at him, but the cheque was cashed without a word. The unfortunate part of it was that in returning to his cab he had encountered an acquaintance both of his own and of the spendthrift soldier, and had been greeted evidently in the latter capacity.

"It was a jolly difficult little moment, Bunny. I had to say there was some mistake, and I had to remember to say it in a manner equally unlike my own and the other beggar's! But all's well that ends well; and if you'll do exactly what I tell you I think we may flatter ourselves that a happy issue is at last in sight."

"What am I to do now?" I asked with some misgiving.

"Clear out of this, Bunny, and wait for me in town. You've done jolly well, old fellow, and so have I in my own department of the game. Everything's in order, down to those fifteen hundred guineas which are now concealed about my person in as hard cash as I can carry. I've seen old Garland and given him back his promissory note myself, with Levy's undertaking about the mortgage. It was a pretty trying interview, as you can understand; but I couldn't help wondering what the poor old boy would say if he dreamt what sort of pressure I've been applying on his behalf! Well, it's all over now except our several exits from the surreptitious stage. I can't make mine without our sleeping partner, but you would really simplify matters, Bunny, by not waiting for us."

There was a good deal to be said for such a course, though it went not a little against my grain. Raffles had changed his clothes and had a bath in town, to say nothing of his luncheon. I was by this time indescribably dirty and dishevelled, besides feeling fairly famished now that mental relief allowed a thought for one's lower man. Raffles had foreseen my plight, and had actually prepared a way of escape for me by the front door in broad daylight. I need not recapitulate the elaborate story he had told the caretaking gardener across the road; but he had borrowed the gardener's keys as a probable purchaser of the property, who had to meet his builder and a business friend at the house during the course of the afternoon. I was to be the builder, and in that capacity to give the gardener an ingenious message calculated to leave Raffles and Levy in uninterrupted possession until my return. And of course I was never to return at all.

The whole thing seemed to me a super-subtle means to a far simpler end than the one we had achieved by stealth in the dead of the previous night. But it was Raffles all over and I ultimately acquiesced, on the understanding that we were to meet again in the Albany at seven o'clock, preparatory to dining somewhere in final celebration of the whole affair.

But much was to happen before seven o'clock, and it began happening. I shook the dust of that derelict tower from my feet; for one of them trod on something at the darkest point of the descent; and the thing went tinkling down ahead on its own account, until it lay shimmering in the light on a lower landing, where I picked it up.

Now I had not said much to Raffles about my hitherto inexplicable experience with the revolver, when I thought it had gone through the banisters, but found it afterwards in my hand. Raffles said it would not have gone through, that I must have been all but over the banisters myself when I grasped the butt as it protruded through them on the level of the floor. This he said (like many another thing) as though it made an end of the matter. But it was not the end of the matter in my own mind; and now I could have told him what the explanation was, or at least to what conclusion I had jumped. I had half a mind to climb all the way up again on purpose to put him in the wrong upon the point. Then I remembered how anxious he had seemed to get rid of me, and for other reasons also I decided to let him wait a bit for his surprise.

Meanwhile my own plans were altered, and when I had delivered my egregious message to the gardener across the road, I sought the nearest shops on my way to the nearest station; and at one of the shops I got me a clean collar, at another a tooth-brush; and all I did at the station was to utilise my purchases in the course of such scanty toilet as the lavatory accommodation would permit.

A few minutes later I was inquiring my way to a house which it took me another twenty or twenty-five to find.

XVII

A Secret Service

This house also was on the river, but it was very small bricks-and-mortar compared with the other two. One of a semi-detached couple built close to the road, with narrow strips of garden to the river's brim, its dingy stucco front and its green Venetian blinds conveyed no conceivable attraction beyond that of a situation more likely to prove a drawback three seasons out of the four. The wooden gate had not swung home behind me before I was at the top of a somewhat dirty flight of steps, contemplating blistered paint and ground glass fit for a bathroom window, and listening to the last reverberations of an obsolete type of bell. There was indeed something oppressively and yet prettily Victorian about the riparian retreat to which Lady Laura Belsize had retired in her impoverished widowhood.

It was not for Lady Laura that I asked, however, but for Miss Belsize, and the almost slatternly maid really couldn't say whether Miss Belsize was in or whether she wasn't. She might be in the garden, or she might be on the river. Would I step inside and wait a minute? I would and did, but it was more minutes than one that I was kept languishing in an interior as dingy as the outside of the house. I had time to take the whole thing in. There were massive remnants of deservedly unfashionable furniture. The sofa I can still see in my mind's eye, and the steel fire-irons, and the crystal chandelier. An aged and gigantic Broadwood occupied nearly half the room; and in a cheap frame thereon, inviting all sorts of comparisons and contrasts, stood a full-length portrait of Camilla Belsize resplendent in contemporary court kit.

I was still studying that frankly barbaric paraphernalia—the feather, the necklace, the coiled train—and wondering what noble kinsman had come to the rescue for the great occasion, and why Camilla should have looked so bored with her finery, when the door opened and she herself entered—not even very smartly dressed—and looking anything but bored, although I say it.

But she did seem astonished, anxious, indignant, reproachful, and to my mind still more nervous and distressed, though this hardly showed through the loopholes of her pride. And as for her white serge coat and skirt, they looked as though they had seen considerable service on the river, and I immediately perceived that one of the large enamel buttons was missing from the coat.

Up to that moment, I may now confess, I had been suffering from no slight nervous anxiety of my own. But all qualms were lost in sheer excitement when I spoke.

"You may well wonder at this intrusion," I began. "But I thought this must be yours, Miss Belsize."

And from my waistcoat pocket I produced the missing button of enamel.

"Where did you find it?" inquired Miss Belsize, with an admirably slight increase of astonishment in voice and look. "And how did you know it was mine?" came quickly in the next breath.

"I didn't know," I answered. "I guessed. It was the shot of my life!"

"But you don't say where you found it?"

"In an empty house not far from here."

She had held her breath; now I felt it like the lightest zephyr. And quite unconsciously I had retained the enamel button.

"Well, Mr. Manders? I'm very much obliged to you. But may I have it back again?"

I returned her property. We had been staring at each other all the time. I stared still harder as she repeated her perfunctory thanks.

"So it was you!" I said, and was sorry to see her looking purposely puzzled at that, but thankful when the reckless light outshone all the rest in those chameleon eyes of hers.

"Who did you think it was?" she asked me with a frosty little smile.

"I didn't know if it was anybody at all. I didn't know what to think," said I, quite candidly. "I simply found his pistol in my hand."

"Whose pistol?"

"Dan Levy's."

"Good!" she said grimly. "That makes it all the better."

"You saved my life."

"I thought you had taken his—and I'd collaborated!"

There was not a tremor in her voice; it was cautious, eager, daring, intense, but absolutely her own voice now.

"No," I said, "I didn't shoot the fellow, but I made him think I had."

"You made me think so too, until I heard what you said to him."

"Yet you never made a sound yourself."

"I should think not! I made myself scarce instead."

"But, Miss Belsize, I shall go perfectly mad if you don't tell me how you happened to be there at all!"

"Don't you think it's for you to tell me that about yourself and—all of you?"

"Oh, I don't mind which of us fires first!" said I, excitedly.

"Then I will," she said at once, and took me to the dreadful sofa at the inner end of the room, and sat down as though it were the most ordinary experience she had to relate. Nor could I believe the things that had really happened, and all so recently, as we talked them over in that commonplace environment of faded gentility. There was a window behind us, overlooking the ribbon of lawn and the cord of gravel, and the bunch of willows that hedged them from the Thames. It all looked unreal to me, unreal in its very realism as the scene of our incredible conversation.

"You know what happened the other afternoon—I mean the day they couldn't play," began Miss Belsize, "because you were there; and though you didn't stay to hear all that came out afterwards, I expect you know everything now. Mr. Raffles would be sure to tell you; in fact, I heard poor dear Mr. Garland give him leave. It's a dreadful story from every point of view. Nobody comes out of it with flying colours, but what nice person could cope with a horrid money-lender? Mr. Raffles, perhaps—if you call him nice!"

I said that was about the worst thing I called him. I mentioned some of the other things. Miss Belsize listened to them with exemplary patience.

"Well," she resumed, "he was quite nice about this. I will say that for him. He said he knew Mr. Levy pretty well, and would see what could be done. But he spoke like an executioner who was going to see what could be done with the condemned man! And all the time I was wondering what had been done already at Carlsbad—what exactly that horrid creature meant when he was talking *at* Mr. Raffles before us all. Well, of course, I knew what he meant us to think he meant; but was there, could there be, anything in it?"

Miss Belsize looked at me as though she expected an answer, only to stop me the moment I opened my mouth to speak.

"I don't want to know, Mr. Manders! Of course you know all about Mr. Raffles"—there was a touch of feeling in this—"but it's nothing to me, though in this case I should certainly have been on his side. You said yourself that it could only have been a practical joke, if there was anything in it at all, and so I tried to think in spite of those horrid men who were following him about at Lord's, even in spite of the way he vanished with them after him. But he never came near the match again—though he had travelled all the way from Carlsbad to see it! Why had he ever been there? What had he really done there? And what could he possibly do to rescue anybody from Mr. Levy, if he himself was already in Levy's power?"

"You don't know Raffles," said I, promptly enough this time. "He never was in any man's power for many minutes. I would back him to save the most desperate situation you could devise."

"You mean by some desperate deed? That's what I feared," declared Miss Belsize, rather strenuously. "Something really had happened at Carlsbad; something worse was by way of happening next. For Teddy's sake," she whispered, "and his poor father's!"

I agreed that old Raffles stuck at nothing for his friends, and Miss Belsize again said that was what she had feared. Her tone had completely altered about Raffles, as well it might. I thought it would have broken with gratitude when she spoke of the unlucky father and son.

"And I was right!" she exclaimed, with that other kind of feeling to which I found it harder to put a name. "I came home miserable from the match on Saturday—"

"Though Teddy had done so well!" I was fool enough to interject.

"I couldn't help thinking about Mr. Raffles," replied Camilla, with a flash of her frank eyes, "and wondering, and wondering, what had happened. And then on Sunday I saw him on the river."

"He didn't tell me."

"He didn't know I recognised him; he was disguised—absolutely!" said Camilla Belsize under her breath. "But he couldn't disguise himself from me," she added as though glorying in her perspicacity.

"Did you tell him so, Miss Belsize?"

"Not I, indeed! I didn't speak to him; it was no business of mine. But there he was, at the bottom of Mr. Levy's garden, having a good look at the boathouse when nobody was about. Why? What could his object be? And why disguise himself? I thought of the affair at Carlsbad, and I felt certain that something of the kind was going to happen again!"

"Well?"

"What could I do? Should I do anything at all? Was it any business of mine? You may imagine the way I cross-questioned myself, and you may imagine the crooked answers I got! I won't bore you with the psychology of the thing; it's pretty obvious after all. It was not so much a case of doing the best as of knowing the worst. All day yesterday there were no developments of any sort, and there was no sign of Mr. Raffles; nothing had happened in the night, or we should have heard of it; but that made me all the more certain that something or other would happen last night. The week's grace was nearly up—you know what I mean—their last week at their own house. If anything was to be done, it was about time, and I knew Mr. Raffles was going to do something. I wanted to know what—that was all."

"Quite right, too!" I murmured. But I doubt if Miss Belsize heard me; she was in no need of my encouragement or my approval. The old light—her own light—the reckless light—was burning away in her brilliant eyes!

"The night before," she went on, "I hardly slept a wink; last night I preferred not to go to bed at all. I told you I sometimes did weird things that astonished the natives of these suburban shores. Well, last night, if it wasn't early this morning, I made my weirdest effort yet. I have a canoe, you know; just now I almost live in it. Last night I went out unbeknowns after midnight, partly to reassure myself, partly—I beg your pardon, Mr. Manders?"

"I didn't speak."

"Your face shouted!"

"I'd rather you went on."

"But if you know what I'm going to say?"

Of course I knew, but I dragged it from her none the less. The nebulous white-shirted figure in the canoe, that had skimmed past Dan Levy's frontage as we were trying to get him aboard his own pleasure-boat, and again past the empty house when we were in the act of disembarking him there, that figure was the trim and slim one now at my side. She had seen us—searched for us—each time. Our voices she had heard and recognised; only our actions, or rather that midnight deed of ours, had she misinterpreted. She would not admit it to me, but I still believe she feared it was a dead body that we had shipped at dead of night to hide away in that desolate tower.

Yet I cannot think she thought it in her heart. I rather fancy (what she indeed averred) that some vague inkling of the truth flashed across her at least as often as that monstrous hypothesis. But know she must; therefore, after boldly ascertaining that nothing was known of the master's whereabouts at Levy's house, but that no uneasiness was entertained on his account, this young woman, true to the audacity which I had seen in her eyes from the first, had taken the still bolder step of landing on the rank lawn and entering the empty tower to discover its secret, for herself. Her stealthy step upon the spiral stair had been the signal for my mortal struggle with Dan Levy. She had heard the whole, and even seen a little of that; in fact, she had gathered enough from Levy's horrible imprecations to form later a rough but not incorrect impression of the situation between him and Raffles and me. As for the moneylender's language, it was with a welcome gleam of humour that Miss Belsize assured me she had "gone too straight to hounds" in her time to be as completely paralysed by it as her mother's neighbours might have been. And as for the revolver, it had fallen at her feet, and first she thought I was going to follow it over the banisters, and before she could think again she had restored the weapon to my wildly clutching hand!

"But when you fired I felt a murderess," she said. "So you see I misjudged you for the second time."

If I am conveying a dash of flippancy in our talk, let me earnestly declare that it was hardly even a dash. It was but a wry and rueful humour on the girl's part, and that only towards the end, but I can promise my worst critic that I was never less facetious in my life. I was thinking in my heavy way that I had never looked into such eyes as these, so bold, so sad, so merry with it all! I was thinking that I had never listened to such a voice, or come across recklessness and sentiment so harmonised, save also in her eyes! I was thinking that there never was a girl to touch Camilla Belsize, or a man either except A. J. Raffles! And yet—

And yet it was over Raffles that she took all the wind from my sails, exactly as she had done at Lord's, only now she did it at parting, and sent me off into the dusk a slightly puzzled and exceedingly exasperated man.

"Of course," said Camilla at her garden gate, "of course you won't repeat a word of what I've told you, Mr. Manders?"

"You mean about your adventures last night and to-day?" said I, somewhat taken aback.

"I mean every single thing we've talked about!" was her sweeping reply. "Not a syllable must go an inch further; otherwise I shall be very sorry I ever spoke to you."

As though she had come and confided in me of her own accord! But I passed that, even if I noticed it at the time.

"I won't tell a soul, of course," I said, and fidgeted. "That is—except—I suppose you don't mind—"

"I do! There must be no exceptions."

"Not even old Raffles?"

"Mr. Raffles least of all!" cried Camilla Belsize, with almost a forked flash from those masterful eyes. "Mr. Raffles is the last person in the world who must ever know a single thing."

"Not even that it was you who absolutely saved the situation for him and me?" I asked, wistfully; for I much wanted these two to think better of each other; and it had begun to look as though I had my wish, so far as Camilla was concerned, while I had only to tell Raffles everything to make him her slave for life. But now she was adamant on the point, adamant heated in some hidden flame.

"It's rather hard lines on me, Mr. Manders, if because I go and get excited, and twist off a button in my excitement, as I suppose I must have done—unless it's a judgment on me—it's rather hard lines if you give me away when I never should have given myself away to you!"

This was unkind. It was still more unfair in view of the former passage between us to the same tune. I was evidently getting no credit for my very irksome fidelity. I helped myself to some at once.

"You gave yourself away to me at Lord's all right," said I, cheerfully. "And I never let out a word of that."

"Not even to Mr. Raffles?" she asked, with a quick unguarded intonation that was almost wistful.

"Not a word," was my reply. "Raffles has no idea you noticed anything, much less how keen you were for me to warn him."

Miss Belsize looked at me a moment with civil war in her splendid eyes. Then something won—I think it was only her pride—and she was holding out her hand.

"He must never know a word of this either," said she, firmly as at first. "And I hope you'll forgive me for not trusting you quite as I always shall for the future."

"I'll forgive you everything, Miss Belsize, except your dislike of dear old Raffles!"

I had spoken quite earnestly, keeping her hand; she drew it away as I made my point.

"I don't dislike him," she answered in a strange tone; but with a stranger stress she added, "I don't *like* him either."

And even then I could not see what the verb should have been, or why Miss Belsize should turn away so quickly in the end, and snatch her eyes away quicker still.

I saw them, and thought of her, all the way back to the station, but not an inch further. So I need no sympathy on that score. If I did, it would have been just the same that July evening, for I saw somebody else and had something else to think about from the moment I set foot upon the platform. It was the wrong platform. I was about to cross by the bridge when a down train came rattling in, and out jumped a man I knew by sight before it stopped.

The man was Mackenzie, the incorrigibly Scotch detective whom we had met at Milchester Abbey, who I always thought had kept an eye on Raffles ever since. He was across the platform before the train pulled up, and I did what Raffles would have done in my place. I ran after him.

"Ye ken Dan Levy's hoose by the river?" I heard him babble to his cabman, with wilful breadth of speech. "Then drive there, mon, like the deevil himsel'!"

XVIII

THE DEATH OF A SINNER

What was I to do? I knew what Raffles would have done; he would have outstripped Mackenzie in his descent upon the moneylender, beaten the cab on foot most probably, and dared Dan Levy to denounce him to the detective. I could see a delicious situation, and Raffles conducting it inimitably to a triumphant issue. But I was not Raffles, and what was more I was due already at his chambers in the Albany. I must have been talking to Miss Belsize by the hour together; to my horror I found it close upon seven by the station clock; and it was some minutes past when I plunged into the first up train. Waterloo was reached before eight, but I was a good hour late at the Albany, and Raffles let me know it in his shirt-sleeves from the window.

"I thought you were dead, Bunny!" he muttered down as though he wished I were. I scaled his staircase at two or three bounds, and began all about Mackenzie in the lobby.

"So soon!" says Raffles, with a mere lift of the eyebrows. "Well, thank God, I was ready for him again."

I now saw that Raffles was not dressing, though he had changed his clothes, and this surprised me for all my breathless preoccupation. But I had the reason at a glance through the folding-doors into his bedroom. The bed was cumbered with clothes and an open suit-case. A Gladstone bag stood strapped and bulging; a travelling rug lay ready for rolling up, and Raffles himself looked out of training in his travelling tweeds.

"Going away?" I exclaimed.

"Rather!" said he, folding a smoking jacket. "Isn't it about time after what you've told me?"

"But you were packing before you knew!"

"Then for God's sake go and do the same yourself!" he cried, "and don't ask questions now. I was beginning to pack enough for us both, but you'll have time to shove in a shirt and collar of your own if you jump straight into a hansom. I'll take the tickets, and we'll meet on the platform at five to nine."

"What platform, Raffles?"

"Charing Cross. Continental train."

E.W. HORNUNG

"But where the deuce do you think of going?"

"Australia, if you like! We'll discuss it in our flight across Europe."

"Our flight!" I repeated. "What has happened since I left you, Raffles?"

"Look here, Bunny, you go and pack!" was all my answer from a savage face, as I was fairly driven to the door. "Do you realise that you were due here one golden hour ago, and have I asked what happened to you? Then don't you ask rotten questions that there's no time to answer. I'll tell you everything in the train, Bunny."

And my name at the end in a different voice, and his hand for an instant on my shoulder as I passed out, were my only consolation for his truly terrifying behaviour, my only comfort and reassurance of any kind, until we really were off by the night mail from Charing Cross.

Raffles was himself again by that time, I was thankful to find, nor did he betray that dread or expectation of pursuit which would have tallied with his previous manner. He merely looked relieved when the Embankment lights ran right and left in our wake. I remember one of his remarks, that they made the finest necklace in the world when all was said, and another that Big Ben was the Koh-i-noor of the London lights. But he had also a quizzical eye upon the paper bag from which I was endeavouring to make a meal at last. And more than once he wagged his head with a humorous admixture of reproof and sympathy; for with shamefaced admissions and downcast pauses I was allowing him to suppose I had been drinking at some riverside public-house instead of hurrying up to town, but that the *rencontre* with Mackenzie had served to sober me.

"Poor Bunny! We won't pursue the matter any further; but I do know where we both should have been between seven and eight. It was as nice a little dinner as I ever ordered in my life. And to think that we never turned up to eat a bite of it!"

"Didn't *you*?" I queried, and my sense of guilt deepened to remorse as Raffles shook his head.

"No fear, Bunny! I wanted to see you safe and sound. That was what made me so stuffy when you did turn up."

Loud were my lamentations, and earnest my entreaties to Raffles to share the contents of my paper bag; but not he. To replace such a feast as he had ordered with sandwiches and hard-boiled eggs would be worse than going healthily hungry for once; it was all very well for me who knew not what I had missed. Not that Raffles was hungry by his own accounts; he had merely fancied a little dinner, more after my heart than his, for our last on British soil.

This, and the way he said it, brought me back to the heart of things; for beneath his frothy phrases I felt that the wine of life was bitter to his taste. His gayety now afforded no truer criterion to his real feelings than had his petulance at the Albany. What had happened since our parting in that fatal tower, to make this wild flight necessary without my news, and whither in all earnest were we to fly?

"Oh, nothing!" said Raffles, in unsatisfactory answer to my first question. "I thought you would have seen that we couldn't clear out too soon after restoring poor Shylock, like our brethren in the song, 'to his friends and his relations.'"

"But I thought you had something else for him to sign?"

"So I had, Bunny."

"What was that?"

"A plain statement of all he had suborned me to do for him, and what he had given me for doing it," said Raffles, as he lit a Sullivan from his last easeful. "One might almost call it a receipt for the letter I stole and he destroyed."

"And did he sign that?"

"I insisted on it for our protection."

"Then we are protected, and yet we cut and run?"

Raffles shrugged his shoulders as we hurtled between the lighted platforms of Herne Hill.

"There's no immunity from a clever cove like that, Bunny, unless you send him to another world or put the thick of this one between you. He may hold his tongue about the last twenty-four hours—I believe he will—but that needn't prevent him from setting old Mackenzie to watch us day and night. So we are not going to stay to be watched. We are starting off round the world for a change. Before we get very far Mr. Shylock may be in the jug himself; that accursed letter won't be the only incriminating thing against him, you take my word. Then we can come back trailing clouds of glory, and blowing clouds of Sullivan. Then we can have our *secondes noces*—meaning second knocks, Bunny, and more power to our elbows when we get them!"

But I was not convinced. There was something else at the bottom of this sudden impulse and its inconceivably sudden execution. Why had he never told me of this plan? Well, because it had never become one until after the morning's work at Levy's bank, in itself a reason for being out of the way, as I myself admitted. But he would have told me if only I had turned up at seven: he had never meant to give me time for much packing, added Raffles, as he was anxious that neither of us should leave the impression that we had gone far afield.

I thought this was childish, and treating me like a child, to which, however, I was used; but more than ever did I feel that Raffles was not being frank with me, that he for one was making good his escape from something or somebody besides Dan Levy. And in the end he admitted that this was so. But we had not dashed through Sitting-bourne and Faversham before I wormed my way to about the last discovery that I expected to make concerning A. J. Raffles.

"What an inquisitor you are, Bunny!" said he, putting down an evening paper that he had only just taken up. "Can't you see that this whole show has been no ordinary one for me? I've been fighting for a crowd I rather love. Their battle has got on my nerves as none of my own ever did; and now it's won I honestly funk their gratitude as much as anything."

That was another hard saying to swallow; and yet, as Raffles said it, I knew it to be true. He was looking me full in the face in the ample light of the first-class compartment, which we of course had to ourselves. Some softening influence seemed to have been at work upon him; he looked resolute as ever, but full of regret, than which nothing was rarer in A.J.

"I suppose," said I, "that poor old Garland has treated you to a pretty good dose already?"

"Yes, Bunny; that he has."

"And well he may, and well may Teddy and Camilla Belsize!"

"But I couldn't do with it from them," said Raffles, with quite a bitter little laugh. "Teddy wasn't there, of course; he's up north for that rotten match the team play nowadays against Liverpool. But the game's fizzling, he'll be home to-morrow, and I simply can't face him and his Camilla. He'll be a married man before we see him again," added Raffles, getting hold of his evening paper once more.

"Is that to come off so soon?"

"The sooner the better," said Raffles, strangely.

"You're not quite happy about it," said I, with execrable tact, I know, and yet deliberately, because his view of this marriage had always puzzled me.

"I'm happy as long as they are," responded Raffles, not without a laugh at his own meritorious sentiment. "I only wish," he sighed, "that they were both absolutely worthy of each other!"

"And you don't think they are?"

"No, I don't."

"You think such a lot of young Garland?"

"I'm very fond of him, Bunny."

"But you see his faults?"

"I've always seen them; they're not full-fathom-five like mine!"

"Yet you think she's not good enough for him?"

"Not good enough—she?" and he stopped himself at that. But his voice was enough for me; the unspoken antithesis was stronger than words could have made it. Scales fell from my eyes. "Where on earth did you get that idea?"

"I thought it was yours, A.J."

"But why?"

"You seemed to disapprove of the engagement from the first."

"So I did, after what poor Teddy had been up to in his extremity! I may as well be honest about that now. It was all right in a pal of ours, Bunny, but all wrong in the man who dreamt of marrying Camilla Belsize."

"Yet you have just been moving heaven and hell to make it possible for them to marry after all!"

Raffles made another attempt upon his paper. I marvel now that he let me catechise him as I was doing. But the truth had just dawned upon me, and I simply had to see it whole as the risen sun, whereas Raffles seemed under no such passionate necessity to keep it to himself.

"Teddy's all right," said he, inconsistently. "He'll never try anything of the kind again; he's had a lesson for life. Besides, I don't often take my hand from the plough, as you ought to know. Bunny. It was I who brought those two together. But it was none of my mundane business to put them asunder again."

"It was you who brought them together?" I repeated insidiously.

"More or less, Bunny. It was at some cricket week, if it wasn't two weeks running; they were pals already, but she and I were greater pals before the first week was over."

"And yet you didn't cut him out!"

"My dear Bunny, I should hope not."

"But you might have done, A.J.; don't tell me you couldn't if you'd tried."

Raffles played with his paper without replying. He was no coxcomb. But neither would he ape an alien humility.

"It wouldn't have been the game, Bunny—won or lost—Teddy or no Teddy: And yet," he added, with pensive candour, "we were getting on like a semi-detached house on fire! I burnt my fingers, I don't mind telling you; if I hadn't been what I am, Bunny, I might have taken my courage in all ten of 'em, and 'put it to the touch, to win or lose it all.'"

"I wish you had," I whispered, as he studied his paper upside down.

"Why, Bunny? What rot you do talk!" he cried, but only with the skin-deep irritation of a half-hearted displeasure.

"She's the only woman I ever met," I went on unguardedly, "who was your mate at heart—in pluck—in temperament!"

"How the devil do you know?" cried Raffles, off his own guard now, and staring in my guilty face.

But I have never denied that I could emulate his presence of mind upon occasion.

"You forget what a lot we saw of each other last Thursday in the rain."

"Did she talk about me then?"

"A little."

"Had she her knife in me, Bunny?"

"Well—yes—a little!"

Raffles smiled stoically: it was a smile of duty done and odds well damned.

"Up to the hilt, Bunny, up to the hilt is what you mean. I stuck it in for her. It's easily done, and it needed doing, for my sake if not for hers. Sooner or later I should have choked her off, so the sooner the better. You play them false, you cut a dance, you let them down over something that doesn't matter, and they'll never give you a dog's chance over anything that does! I got her to write and never answered. What do you think of that for a cavalier swine? I said I'd call before I went abroad, and only wired to say sorry I couldn't. I don't say it would or could have been all right otherwise; but you see it was all right for Teddy before I got back! Which was as it was to be. She would hardly look at me at first last week; but, Bunny, she wasn't above looking when that old Shylock was playing at giving me away before them all. She looked at him, and she looked at me, and I've got one of the looks she gave him, and another that she never meant me to see, bottled in my blackguard heart forever!"

Raffles looked dim to me across the narrow compartment; but there was no nonsense in his look or voice. I longed to tell him all I knew, all that she had said to me and he had unwittingly interpreted; that she loved him, as now at last I knew she did; but I had given her my word, and after all it was a word to keep for both their sakes as well as for its own.

"You were made for each other, you two!"

That was all I said, and Raffles only laughed.

"All the more reason to hook it round the world, Bunny, before there's a dog's chance of our meeting again."

He opened his paper the proper way up at last. The train rushed on with flying sparks, and flying lights along the line. We were getting nearer Dover now. My next brilliant remark was that I could "smell the sea." Raffles let it pass; he had been talking of the close-of-play scores in the stop-press column, and I thought he was studying them rather silently. Or perhaps he was not studying them at all, but still thinking of Camilla Belsize, and the look from those brave bright eyes that she had never meant him to see. Then, suddenly, I perceived that his forehead was glistening white and wet in the lamplight.

"What is it, Raffles? What's the matter?"

He reversed his paper with a shaky hand, and thrust it upon me without a word, merely pointing out four or five ill-printed lines of latest news. This was the item that danced before my eyes:

TRAGIC DEATH OF FAMOUS MONEYLENDER

Mr. Daniel Levy, the financier, reported shot dead at front gates of his residence in Thames Valley at 5.30 this afternoon, by unknown man who made good his escape.

I looked up into a ghastly face.

"It was half-past five when I left him, Bunny!"

"You left him—"

I could not ask it. But the ghastly face had given me a ghastlier thought.

"As well as you are, Bunny!" so Raffles completed my sentence. "Do you think I'd leave him for dead at his own gates?"

Of course I denied the thought; but it had come to haunt me none the less; for if I had sailed so near such a deed, what about Raffles under equal provocation? And what such motive for the very flight that we were making with but a moment's preparation? It all fitted in, except the face and voice of Raffles as they had been while he was speaking of Camilla Belsize; but again, the fatal act would indeed have made him feel that he had lost her, and loosened his tongue upon his loss as something had done without doubt; and as for voice and face, there was no longer in either any lack of the mad excitement of the hunted man.

"But what were you doing at his gates, A.J.?"

"I saw him home. It was on my way. Why not?"

"And you say you left him at half-past five?"

"I swear it. I looked at my watch, thinking of my train, and my watch is plumb right."

"And you heard no shot as you went on?"

"No—I was hurrying. I even ran. I must have been seen running! And now I'm like Charley's Aunt," he went on with his sardonic laugh, "and bound to stick to it until they catch me by the leg. Now you know what Mackenzie was doing down there! The old hound may be on my track already. There's no going back now."

"Not for an innocent man?"

"Not for such dubious innocence as mine, Bunny! Remember all we've been up to with poor old Levy for the last twenty-four hours."

He paused, remembering everything himself, as I could see; and the human compassion in his face should have been sufficient answer to my vile misgivings. But there was contrition in his look as well, and that was a much rarer sign in Raffles. Rarer still was a glance of alarm almost akin to panic, alike without precedent in my experience of my friend and beyond belief in my reading of his character. But through all there peeped a conscious enjoyment of these new sensations, a very zest in the novelty of fear, which I knew to be at once signally characteristic, and yet compatible either with his story or with my own base dread.

"Nobody need ever know about that," said I, with the certainty that nobody ever would know through the one other who knew already. But Raffles threw cold water upon that poor little flicker of confidence and good hope.

"It's bound to come out, Bunny. They'll start accounting for his last hours on earth, and they'll stick ominously in the first five minutes working backwards. Then I am described as bolting from the scene, then identified with myself, then found to have fled the country! Then Carlsbad, then our first row with him, then yesterday's big cheque; my heavy double finds he was impersonated at the bank; it all comes out bit by bit, and if I'm caught it means that dingy Old Bailey dock on the capital charge!"

"Then I'll be with you," said I, "as accessory before and after the fact. That's one thing!"

"No, no, Bunny! You must shake me off and get back to town. I'll push you out as we slow down through the streets of Dover, and you can put up for the night at the Lord Warden. That's the sort of public place for the likes of us to lie low in, Bunny. Don't forget all my rules when I'm gone."

"You're not going without me, A.J."

"Not even if I did it, Bunny?"

"No; less than ever then!"

Raffles leant across and took my hand. There was a flash of mischief in his eyes, but a very tender light as well.

"It makes me almost wish I were what I do believe you thought I was," said he, "to see you stick to me all the same! But it's about time that we were making the lights of Dover," he added, beating an abrupt retreat from sentiment, even to the length of getting up and looking out as we clattered through a country station. His head was in again before the platform was left behind, a pale face peering into mine, real panic flaring in those altered eyes, like blue lights at sea. "My God, Bunny!" cried Raffles. "I believe Dover's as far as I shall ever get!"

"Why? What's the matter now?"

"A head sticking out of the next compartment but one!"

"Mackenzie's?"

"Yes!"

I had seen it in his face.

"After us already?"

"God knows! Not necessarily; they watch the ports after a big murder."

"Swagger detectives from Scotland Yard?"

Raffles did not answer; he had something else to do. Already he was turning his pockets inside out. A false beard rolled off the seat.

"That's for you," he said as I picked it up. "I'll finish making you up." He was busy on himself in one of the oblong mirrors, kneeling on the cushions to be near his work. "If it's a scent at all it must be a pretty hot one, Bunny, to have landed him in the very train and coach! But it mayn't be as bad as it looked at first sight. He can't have much to go upon yet. If he's only going to shadow us while they find out more at home, we shall give him the slip all right."

"Do you think he saw you?"

"Looking out? No, thank goodness, he was looking toward Dover too."

"But before we started?"

"No, Bunny, I don't believe he came aboard before Cannon Street. I remember hearing a bit of a fuss there. But our blinds were down, thank God!"

They were all down now, but by our decreasing speed I felt that we were already gliding over level crossings to the admiration of belated townsfolk waiting at the gates. Raffles turned from his mirror, and I from mine, simultaneously; and even to my initiated eye it was not Raffles at all, but another noble scamp who even in those days before the war was the observed of all observers about town.

"It's ever so much better than anonymous disguises," said Raffles, as he went to work upon me with his pocket make-up box and his lightning touch. "I was always rather like him, and I tried him on yesterday with such success at the bank that I certainly can't do better to-night. As for you, Bunny, if you slouch your hat and stick your beard in your bread basket, you ought to pass for a poor relation or a disreputable dun. But here we are, my lad, and now for Meester Mackenzie o' Scoteland Yarrd!"

The gaunt detective was in fact the first person we beheld upon the pier platform; raw-boned, stiff-jointed, and more than middle-aged, he must nevertheless have jumped out once again before the train stopped, and that almost on top of a diminutive telegraph boy, who was waiting while the old hound read his telegram with one eye and watched emerging passengers with both. Whether we should have passed him unobserved I cannot say. We could but have tried; but Raffles preferred to grasp the nettle and salute Mackenzie with a pleasant nod.

"Good evening, my lord!" says the Scotchman with a canny smirk.

"I can guess why you're down here," says Raffles, actually producing a palpable Sullivan under the nose of the law.

"Is that a fact?" inquires the other, oiling the rebuff with deferential grin.

"And I mustn't stand between you and poor Dan Levy's murderer," adds my lord, nodding finally, when Mackenzie steps after him to my horror. But it is only to show Raffles his telegram. And he does not follow us on board.

Neither did our disguises accompany our countenances across the Channel. It was at dead of night on the upper deck (whence all but us had fled) that Raffles showed me how to doff my beard and still look as though I had merely buttoned it inside my overcoat; meanwhile his own moustachios and imperial were disappearing by discreet degrees; and at last he told me why, though not by any means without pressing.

"I'm only afraid you'll want to turn straight back from Calais, Bunny!"

"Oh, no, I shan't."

"You'll come with me round the world, so to speak?"

"To its uttermost ends, A. J.!"

"You do know now who it really is that I don't want to see again just yet?"

"Yes. I know. Now tell me what Mackenzie told you."

"It was all in the wire he showed me," said Raffles. "The wire was to say that the murderer of Dan Levy had given himself up to the police!"

Profane expletives flew from my lips; those of much holier men might have been no less unguardedly emphatic in the self-same circumstances.

"But who was it?"

"I could have told you all along if you hadn't suspected me."

"It wasn't a suspicion, Raffles. It was never more than a dread, and I didn't even dread it in my heart of hearts. Do tell me now."

Raffles watched the red end of a ruined Sullivan make a fine trajectory as it flew to leeward between sea and stars.

"It was that poor unlucky little alien who was waiting for him the other morning in Jermyn Street, and again last night near his own garden gate. That's where he got him in the end. But it wasn't a shooting case at all, Bunny; that's why I never heard anything. It was a case of stabbing in accordance with the best traditions of the Latin races."

"God forgive both poor devils!" said I at last.

"And other two," said Raffles, "who have rather more to be forgiven."

XIX

Apologia

On one of the worst days of last year, to wit the first day of the Eton and Harrow match, I had turned into the Hamman, in Jermyn Street, as the best available asylum for wet boots that might no longer enter any club. Mine had been removed by a little pinchbeck oriental in the outer courts, and I wandered within unpleasantly conscious of a hole in one sock, to find myself by no means the only obvious refugee from the rain. The bath was in fact inconveniently crowded. But at length I found a divan to suit me in an upstairs alcove. I had the choice indeed of more than one; but in spite of my antecedents I am fastidious about my cooling companions in a Turkish bath, and it was by no accident that I hung my clothes opposite to a newer morning coat and a pair of trousers more decisively creased than my own.

But the coincidence in pickle was no less remarkable. In ensuing stages of physical devastation one had dim glimpses of a not unfamiliar, reddish countenance; but with the increment of years it has been my lot to contract short sight as well as incipient obesity, and in the hot rooms my glasses lose their grip upon my nose. So it was not until I lay swathed upon my divan that I recognised E.M. Garland in the fine fresh-faced owner of the nice clothes opposite mine. A tawny moustache rather spoilt him as Phoebus, and there was a hint of old gold about the shaven jaw and chin; but I never saw better looks of the unintellectual order; and the amber eye was as clear as ever, the great strong wicket-keeper's hand unexpectedly hearty, when recognition dawned on Teddy in his turn.

He spoke of Raffles without hesitation or reserve, and of me and my Raffles writings as though there was nothing reprehensible in one or the other, displaying indeed a flattering knowledge of those pious memorials.

"But of course I take them with a grain of salt," said Teddy Garland; "you don't make me believe you were either of you such desperate dogs as all that. I can't see you climbing ropes or squirming through scullery windows—even for the fun of the thing!" he added with somewhat tardy tact.

It is certainly rather hard to credit now. I felt that after all there was something to be said for being too fat at forty, and that Teddy Garland had said it excellently.

"Now," he continued, "if only you would give us the row between Raffles and Dan Levy, I mean the whole battle royal that A.J. fought and won for me and my poor father, that would be something like! The world would see the sort of chap he really was."

"I am afraid it would have to see the sort of chaps we all were just then," said I, as I still think with exemplary delicacy; but Teddy lay silent and florid for some time. These athletes have their vanity. But this one rose superior to his.

"Manders," said he, leaving his divan and coming and sitting on the edge of mine, "you have my free leave to give me and mine away to the four winds, if you will tell the truth about that duel, and what Raffles did for the lot of us!"

"Perhaps he did more than you ever knew."

"Put it all in."

"It was a longer duel than you think. He once called it a guerilla duel."

"Then make a book of it."

"But I've written my last word about the old boy."

"Then by George I've a good mind to write it myself!"

This was an awful threat. Happily he lacked the materials, and so I told him. "I haven't got them all myself," I added, only to be politely but openly disbelieved. "I don't know where you were," said I, "all that first day of the match, when it rained."

Garland was beginning to smile when the surprise of my statement got home and changed his face.

"Do you mean to say A.J. never told you?" he cried, still incredulously.

"No; he wouldn't give you away."

"Not even to you—his pal?"

"No. I was naturally curious on the point. But he refused to tell me."

"What a chap!" murmured Teddy, with a tender enthusiasm that made me love him. "What a friend for a fellow! Well, Manders, if you don't write all this I certainly shall. So I may as well tell you where I was."

"I must say it would interest me to know."

My companion resumed his smile where he had left it off. "I wonder if you would ever guess?" he speculated, looking down into my face.

"I don't suppose I should."

"No more do I; not in a month of Sundays; for I spent that day on the very sofa I was on a minute ago!"

I looked at the striped divan opposite. I looked at Teddy Garland sitting on mine. His smile was a little wry with the remnant of his bygone shame; he hurried on before I could find a word.

"You remember that drug I had? Somnol I think it was. That was a risky game to play with any head but one's own; still A.J. was right in thinking I should have been worse without any sleep at all. I should," said Teddy, "but I should have rolled up at Lord's! The beastly stuff put me asleep all right, but it didn't keep me asleep long enough! I was awake before four, heard you both talking in the next room, remembered everything in a flash! But for that flash I should have dropped off again in a minute; but if you remember all I had to remember, Manders, you won't wonder that I lay madly awake all the rest of the night. My head was rotten with sleep, but my heart was in such hell as I couldn't describe to you if I tried."

"I've been there," said I, briefly.

"Well, then, you can imagine my frightful thoughts. Suicide was one; but to get out of that came first, to get away without looking either of you in the face in broad daylight. So I shammed sleep when Raffles looked in, and when you both went out I dressed in five minutes and slunk out too. I had no idea where I was going. I don't remember what brought me down into this street. It may have been my debt to Dan Levy. All I remember is finding myself opposite this place, my head splitting, and the sudden idea that a bath might freshen me up and couldn't make me worse. I remembered A.J. telling me he had once taken six wickets after one. So in I came. I had my bath, and some tea and toast in the hot-rooms; we were all to have a late breakfast together, if you recollect. I felt I should be in plenty of time for that and Lord's— if only I hadn't boiled all the cricket out of me. So I came up here and lay down there. But what I hadn't boiled out was that beastly drug. It got back on me like a boomerang. I closed my eyes for a minute—and it was well on in the afternoon when I awoke!"

Here Teddy interrupted himself to order whiskies and soda of a metropolitan Bashi-Bazouk who happened to pass along the gallery; and to go stumbling over to his pockets, in his swaddling towels, for cigarettes and matches. And the rest of his discourse was less coherent.

"Then I did feel it was a toss-up between my razor and a charge of shot! I had no idea it was raining; if you look up at that coloured skylight, you can't say if it's raining now. There's another sort of hatchway on top of it. Then you hear that fountain tinkling all the time; you don't hear any rain, do you?—It was after three, but I lay till nearly four simply cursing my luck; there was no hurry then. At last I wondered what the papers had to say about me—who was playing in my place, who'd won the toss and all the rest of it. So I had the nerve to send out for one, and what should I see? 'No play at Lord's'—and sudden illness of my poor old father! You know the rest, Manders, because in less than twenty minutes after that we met."

"And I remember thinking how fit you looked," said I. "It was the bath, of course, and the sleep on top of it. But I wonder they let you sleep so long."

"How could they know what I'd been up to?" said Teddy. "I mightn't have had any sleep for a week; it was their business to let me be. But to think of the rain coming on and saving me—for even Raffles couldn't have done it without the rain. That was the great slice of luck—while I was lying right there! And that's why I like to lie there still—for luck rather than remembrance!"

The drinks came; we smoked and sipped. I regretted to find that Teddy was no longer faithful to the only old cigarette. But his loyalty to Raffles won my heart as he had never won it in his youth.

"Give us away to your heart's content," said he; "but give the dear old devil his due at last."

"But who exactly do you mean by 'us'?"

"My father not so much, perhaps, because he's dead and gone; but self and wife as much as ever you like."

"Are you sure Mrs. Garland won't mind?"

"Mind! It was for her he did it all; didn't you know that?"

I didn't know Teddy knew it, and I began to think him a finer fellow than I had supposed.

"Am I to say all I know about that too?" I asked.

"Rather! Camilla and I will both be delighted—so long as you change our names—for we both loved him!" said Teddy Garland.

I wonder if they both forgive me for taking him entirely at his word?

A Note About the Author

Ernest William Hornung (1866–1921) was an English author and poet, best known as a crime writer who often published under his initials, E.W. Hornung. When he was seventeen, Hornung moved to Australia, with the hope that the climate would remedy his poor health. Hornung often referred to this time as one of the best periods of his life, and he based much of his work off an Australian setting. A little over two years later, Hornung returned to England and worked as a journalist during the active period of the infamous serial killer Jack the Ripper, which likely sparked his interest in crime fiction. Hornung married Connie Doyle, the sister of major author Arthur Conan Doyle, in 1893. While the author explored many important themes in his work, the topics of Australia, crime, and cricket were commonly present in his work, signifying Hornung's interest and passion for each.

A Note from the Publisher

Spanning many genres, from non-fiction essays to literature classics to children's books and lyric poetry, Mint Edition books showcase the master works of our time in a modern new package. The text is freshly typeset, is clean and easy to read, and features a new note about the author in each volume. Many books also include exclusive new introductory material. Every book boasts a striking new cover, which makes it as appropriate for collecting as it is for gift giving. Mint Edition books are only printed when a reader orders them, so natural resources are not wasted. We're proud that our books are never manufactured in excess and exist only in the exact quantity they need to be read and enjoyed.

bookfinity™

Discover more of your favorite classics with Bookfinity™.

- Track your reading with custom book lists.
- Get great book recommendations for your personalized Reader Type.
- Add reviews for your favorite books.
- AND MUCH MORE!

Visit **bookfinity.com** and take the fun Reader Type quiz to get started.

Enjoy our classic and modern companion pairings!

Printed in the USA
CPSIA information can be obtained
at www.ICGtesting.com
JSHW082341140824
68134JS00020B/1799